The Ordinary and Extraordinary AUDEN GREENE

Also by Corey Ann Haydu
Eventown
The Someday Suitcase
Rules for Stealing Stars
One Jar of Magic
The Widely Unknown Myth of Apple & Dorothy

The Ordinary and Extraordinary Auden Greene

COREY ANN HAYDU

Quill Tree Books
An Imprint of HarperCollinsPublishers

HarperCollins Children's Books, a division of HarperCollins Publishers,
195 Broadway, New York, NY 10007
HarperCollins Publishers, Macken House, 39/40 Mayor Street Upper,
Dublin 1, D01 C9W8, Ireland

Quill Tree Books is an imprint of HarperCollins Publishers.

The Ordinary and Extraordinary Auden Greene
Copyright © 2026 by Corey Ann Haydu
All rights reserved. Manufactured in Harrisonburg, VA, United States of America. No part of this book may be used or reproduced in any manner whatsoever without written permission except in the case of brief quotations embodied in critical articles and reviews. Without limiting the exclusive rights of any author, contributor, or the publisher of this publication, any unauthorized use of this publication to train generative artificial intelligence (AI) technologies is expressly prohibited. HarperCollins also exercises their rights under Article 4(3) of the Digital Single Market Directive 2019/790 and expressly reserves this publication from the text and data mining exception.

harpercollins.com

Library of Congress Control Number: 2025943553
ISBN 978-0-06-334814-1

Typography by Amy Ryan
25 26 27 28 29 LBC 5 4 3 2 1
First Edition

*To teachers everywhere
and especially those in the NYC public school system—
thank you.*

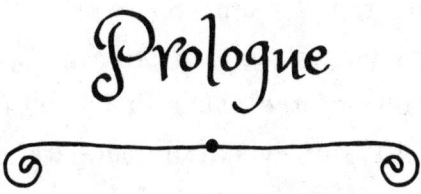

Prologue

They're coming for me.

The dragons—with their heavy, flapping wings and smoky breath and scales as sharp as knives—are coming for me, the way they always come for princesses.

"They can take me instead," Lady Genevive says. "Sorrowfeld doesn't need me. I'm not anyone, I'm not a princess." She is the scared kind of brave—her arms across her chest, her cheeks so pink they look like flowers in bloom, her legs shaking without buckling.

We are in the Northern Tower, my favorite one, up the twistiest stairs with the biggest windows looking out at the kingdom, but now all I can see is smoke and swoops of green-gold dragon tails. There are cries from the townspeople—some of them beg the dragons to let me be. Some loudly declare they'd be better off without me.

"Take her!" they scream. "Spare us!"

I'm shaking now too. My stomach spiraling, my back waterfall-wet, the whole of me wishing I were somewhere else, somewhere simpler. Home.

"I'm not a princess either," I tell Lady Genevive, who is my best friend here. The shape of her is the same as my real best friend—tall and dark-haired and moony-eyed and dimpled. She doesn't hear me over the roars of dragons desperate to capture the very last princess of Sorrowfeld, the one who has remained, the one they didn't take before. Me. Or the me they think I am.

"I'm not a princess," I try again, and she hears this time. She almost ignores it—a wave starting in her hand, a dismissive *of course you are* beginning on her lips. But something stops her. Maybe she sees me at last. Maybe she sees what she's been missing all this time.

I look like her and sound like her and stand in this tower like her and am threatened by dragons like her. But I am not her.

I am not Princess Auden of Sorrowfeld.

I'm just Denny.

The Tale of Dragons True

Denny and Runa, age 7

Sorrowfeld is the best best kingdom ever!!!! There are three princesses in Sorrowfeld. They are so beautiful.

Princesses wear pink.

And tiaras!

They live in towers. They have soft blankets. They have fuzzy pillows.

They dance on pointe. They play the flute. They have braids and buns and makeup.

Princesses have birthstone necklaces. Rubies. Amethysts. Opals. They're really pretty. They are gifts from fairies!

The Tale of Dragons True

Denny, age 11

In Sorrowfeld, there are secrets. Of course there are.

But they won't stay secret forever. If you look, if you really look, you'll see what's been hidden.

Sorrowfeld has dragons and curses and witches living on enchanted lakes. But it is safe. Because its secrets all, eventually, come out.

Chapter 1

Denny Greene
Twenty-Seven Days Before the Swap

In the garden shed, there is one semibroken lawn chair; one sleeping bag that Mom used when she was in college; an abandoned collection in the corner of tiaras, fairy wings, and cardboard castles; two curtains made out of gold-and-silver-striped fabric; and a dozen dragons made of clay, painted in blues and teals and oranges and pale pinks.

The collection of dragons stays the same. The stories we tell about them change depending on our moods. Like everything else, the stories get more complicated every year.

My best friend, Runa, holds one of the dragons in her hand. She strokes its head. "This one wanted to be a sailor," she says. "Before she got turned into a dragon."

"Now she ravages the seas," I add. "Burns the shores. Grabs ships right from the waves and tosses them away."

"Yeah."

Usually, the story continues, the two of us building a history so complicated and dramatic that afternoons turn to evenings, and we grow hungry and tired and forgetful of what else is outside the garden shed. But Runa's *yeah* sounds final, like another way of saying *the end*.

"That's it?" I ask.

"That's it," Runa replies. Lately Runa has been stopping the story before it really begins.

Lately, the world outside the garden shed seems louder—a world of friends with short, swingy haircuts and flared jeans and jokes about teachers I thought we liked, music I thought we hated. A world of science experiments in itchy lab coats in the too-hot science room and field trips to places where wars were fought. Shirts that don't fit right and smudged glasses and makeup I don't know how to wear because Mom fell apart at the exact moment I got curious about how to wear makeup, so she can't teach me how to use it.

I keep waiting to care about the face cream and the haircuts and the jeans and the girls who Runa says are our friends now.

But I still mostly only care about Runa and Broadway

musicals and *The Tale of Dragons True*, a collection of writings and drawings in a leather-bound journal that Dad gave me when I turned seven. The journal is almost full now.

Runa and I invented a kingdom called Sorrowfeld and filled the book with everything we know about it.

It started as a story of princesses, when all we cared about were princesses and castles and sparkly tiaras that we would draw in great detail because Runa's parents said one dress-up tiara was more than enough and my parents always seem to forget everything they might know about me when they go shopping for my birthday. I love books, but they get me ones about regular kids when I want to read about fantastical adventures. They confuse dragons with dinosaurs and get me paleontology kits and brontosaurus stuffies. Sometimes they forget who I am altogether, and I open up a board game or a craft kit, the sort of thing that already has the rules written, that tells you how to play.

But they always knew how to throw a great birthday party.

After Runa and I had written everything we could about the princesses of Sorrowfeld, we got interested in neighboring kingdoms and the sorts of battles that might happen between them. We wrote about fairies that live in the trees and mermaids in the rivers. We even tried writing anthems for Sorrowfeld, imagining what the townspeople might sing when celebrating their royalty. But the songs are never actually very good, and usually we end up turning on a Broadway soundtrack instead—"One Day More" from *Les Mis* or "Ring of Keys" from *Fun Home* or, lately, "Over the Rainbow" from *The Wizard of Oz*, since that is officially the spring musical this year.

This past year, we've been writing mostly about the dragons. They'd always been in the background—Sorrowfeld is a kingdom forever living under the threat of dragons. Their fiery breath even created the holes in the trees where the fairies live. But in our stories, they used to just be smoke and fire, flapping wings, loud growls that made the royals scream. The villains.

This year, though, Runa and I decided that the dragons are actually cursed human beings, sentenced to live life as feared beasts. Having to grieve their former human lives is what made them so mad, so fiery and destructive.

I guess it feels good to know what it is that's making someone so upset. Even if that someone is a dragon.

Runa's holding *The Tale of Dragons True* and I'm adjusting a curtain when she says, in this voice I've never really heard her use, "I sort of want to be a dragon sometimes."

"No one wants to be a dragon," I say with a laugh. Runa and I want to be princesses. We want to be knights and kings and mermaids and unicorns. We understand the dragons now, but we don't want to *be* them. We wrote it all out very, very clearly.

Everyone thought dragons were monsters.

And this is true, if you think humans are monsters.

They are heartbroken to have this curse placed upon them. Horrified to be dragons. They can't stand to remember what used to be. It is simply too painful. So they destroy kingdoms, threaten humans, kill kings and queens and villagers, all to forget about their formerly human hearts, their human pasts, their unlived human futures.

The Tale of Dragons True is written back and forth, half in my handwriting, half in Runa's. There are drawings. Maps. Images that remind us of our kingdom that we've pasted in after finding them online or on book covers or postcards.

We disagree, sometimes, on what is true about Sorrowfeld. About princesses and dragons and witches and fairies. So the book is complicated and wild, a little like Sorrowfeld.

A little like us, lately.

"I guess I mean—dragons get it. You know?" Runa smooths out her hair, even though it looks perfectly smooth to me already. "Sometimes it's better to destroy everything in the past so that you can just be who you are. Like, in third grade I still brought my stuffed unicorn to school. I don't want to remember that."

"Isabelle," I say. Runa still sleeps with her.

"Or, like, our doll dinner party birthday. I wish everyone could forget about that." Runa twirls her new star stud earring. I'm too scared to pierce my ears, but she finally did it, and the blue-silver stars are her favorite pair. She doesn't wear the ones I got her very often—tiny gold crowns that I was sure were the perfect You Got Your Ears Pierced gift.

"But it was so fun." I don't want to forget that party. Mom planned it, making miniature burgers and tiny fries and these little salads served in dishes smaller than the palm of my hand. She tore the spinach leaves up into dime-sized pieces and used an eyedropper to put salad dressing on. We dressed our dolls up in their fanciest clothes, and Mom let us use all her prettiest dresses and jewelry for ourselves, and I can't think of a single reason why Runa would want to forget it. We have a photo of it in a frame right here in the shed, on the windowsill next to Mom's gardening gloves. In it,

Runa is smiling a gap-toothed smile and Mom's wedding gown is falling off me, the heart-shaped birthmark on my shoulder just peeking out.

"Yeah. For little kids. But we aren't little kids. Like, wouldn't you want everyone to forget about the talent show last year?"

Runa and I never talk about the talent show. My heart pounds.

"That's different," I say.

"Sorry. Yeah. I just meant it would be nice for you to get to audition this year without anyone remembering that whole thing."

That whole thing was me choosing to sing "Popular" at the fifth-grade talent show and then completely losing my nerve before ever beginning. I stood up on the stage and the notes played and I tried to sing the first few words, but they came out a whisper, all cracked and throaty and low, and I heard someone laugh. It was Sadie, who was a new girl at the beginning of fifth grade. I remember she looked scared on the first day of fifth grade, but she got unscared really fast, and soon everyone wanted to be like her with her star stud earrings and special silvery bronzer.

Everyone, including Runa. Who didn't like that Sadie laughed, but somehow became her friend anyway.

I ran off the stage that day, looking for Mom, but

Mom was still in her car. She'd never joined the audience. She'd missed the whole thing.

"It's too hard," she'd said. "I need to go home. This is too much."

A lot of things started being too much over the last year or so. Lately, whenever I'm looking for her at a soccer game or a parent night or even at her own office, she's in her car instead, gripping the steering wheel, staring at nothing. Or, more likely, upstairs in bed. Sometimes she's crying. Sometimes she's yelling.

Every once in a while, she's Mom again, flickering into being, watching a movie with me, braiding my hair, asking me who I ate lunch with, just like she used to.

Then she vanishes again.

Sadie won the talent show with her rendition of "Tomorrow" from *Annie*.

I didn't bother telling Mom what had happened with me.

Later, when I sang my song for Runa, pretending the big rock in our backyard was a stage, and she and the birds and squirrels and trees and our collection of dragons were a whole audience, Runa told me, "You would have won, Denny."

So, yes, I'd like to forget the talent show, and it's true that Runa started wearing star stud earrings not long after. But I still wouldn't want to forget that moment when Runa was the whole world, when it was good enough to be spectacular just right there. Just for her.

"Forget I said anything," Runa says now. She opens *The Tale of Dragons True* back up and starts drawing a new dragon, one with pink dragon skin and long, scaly ears. No one has ever been better at drawing dragons than Runa Rossi.

"That one used to be a little girl," I say. "She grew up in Paris. She loved croissants. She was a ballerina."

"Then she fell into the Lake of Leer, outside the witch's castle, and was cursed to be a dragon forever."

I'm relieved we are back in our groove, doing what we do best. "Destroying croissants and ballet shoes and princesses everywhere she goes."

"Desperate to forget the little girl she once was."

"Now a dangerous dragon. Taking down entire kingdoms. Until she truly forgets she was ever a human at all."

"Like all dragons eventually do," Runa concludes.

When it is time to leave the shed, we make sure to close the book. Put the dragon figurines in the toolbox, where tools no longer live. We lock the shed door. Sorrowfeld is our secret. We don't want anyone to come in and see it.

But also—and maybe it sounds silly and Runa

would say it's babyish—we don't want Sorrowfeld and the dragons to escape. Just in case.

Because when the sun is setting and the light in the shed is sort of golden pink and it gets chilly and drafty and shadowy, it feels possible that the things we've been imagining all these years could almost—*almost*—be real. If we aren't careful.

The Tale of Dragons True

Runa and Denny, age 8

Sometimes dragons capture royals from their castles.

No one knows where dragons take them.

It is one of the great mysteries of Sorrowfeld.

Beware, there are many, many mysteries of the kingdom of Sorrowfeld.

Chapter 2

Denny Greene
Eleven Days Before the Swap

The trouble starts while we're hanging out in Runa's bedroom. Runa says she wants the cake to be black and white, when we've always said that at our twelfth birthday, our cake would be purple. We've been making our way through the rainbow since our seventh birthday, when we had a red velvet cake covered in red frosting roses. We've finally arrived at purple, which is obviously one of the best colors, and is definitely, without a doubt, better than plain old black and white.

"And I don't think we should do a dragon," Runa says, without even leaving room for me to argue for the merits of purple frosting. "Let's keep it simple. *Happy Birthday Runa and Auden* on top. That could maybe be in purple. If you're, like, desperate for purple or whatever."

"I'm not desperate for purple," I say, "It's just we did all the other colors in the rainbow. So it's time for purple. And why would it say *Auden*?"

"That's your name."

That's when I realize Runa is writing our plans down in *The Tale of Dragons True*, not in the spiral-bound notebook I took out for birthday planning. I get an uncomfortable jolt, seeing real-life words where there should only be Sorrowfeld stories.

"That's the wrong notebook," I say. "Here." I push the yellow spiral one toward her.

"You don't care, right?" she replies, even though I'm pretty sure she knows I *do* care, and she's always cared too, but now we are on different sides of the caring divide, and it will feel even worse if I say anything else. Lately, there's a tone in her voice that makes me go quiet, that makes me uncertain about things I thought we'd decided together.

We never explicitly said that we would only write about Sorrowfeld in *The Tale of Dragons True* journal, just like we never said we would always have matching green sparkly sunglasses or that we wouldn't ever wear lipstick or that it would always just be the two of us against the world. We didn't say those things because they were so obvious.

But now she's wearing glossy pink lipstick and

contact lenses and her thick dark hair is straighter than it used to be and she's making a list of boring decorations in our beloved book that shouldn't even be here. We've never taken it out of the shed before, but Runa said I should bring it over, so I did, and now she's maybe sort of ruining it.

We aren't supposed to mix real life with Sorrowfeld. It feels wrong. And sort of dangerous, which I don't say to Runa, because I think this new version of Runa would laugh at me.

Plus she's calling me Auden.

"No one calls me Auden." It feels weird to explain my name to my best friend, who knows I have only ever been Denny.

"Maybe they should." Runa shrugs.

"Well, maybe they should call you Queen Elsablue of Isindoralora," I say, but Runa doesn't laugh, doesn't add on to my idea the way she's always done, doesn't call me Queen Nezzledrummer of Agleberry, or demand I draw a picture of her royal bedroom or start writing a story about the dragon that Queen Elsablue defeated in order to remain in her beloved kingdom.

"I just think Auden is pretty. Sort of more mature, you know? Emily didn't even know that was your real name, and she said if you went by Auden, you'd be, like, a whole different person."

"I don't want to be a whole different person," I say, but suddenly I'm not so sure. I scratch my shoulder where my heart-shaped birthmark is. I tuck my hair behind my ears and wonder if that looks mature, too. I wiggle my toes.

"In Sorrowfeld, everything changes when the princesses turn twelve, right? And we're turning twelve. So."

"But not their *names*," I say, not mentioning that it's Runa, not me, who keeps writing in all these rules about everything changing on a princess's twelfth birthday. I sort of want to write about how everything stays the same. Or maybe goes back to how it used to be. I want Sorrowfeld to be better than here.

"Okay. *Happy Birthday Runa and Denny*, then," Runa says, like calling me by my actual name is some huge compromise she's making. "In lavender. The rest of the cake just white with black details."

She doesn't say what the details will be. Not dragons, I guess. Not crowns or castles either, I bet. I look around Runa's bedroom, which used to look an awful lot like mine, and still does, in certain corners. But her bedspread is black-and-white-striped now. There's a mirror hanging over her dresser that replaced one of our illustrations of a princess in the process of transforming into a dragon, a tail growing out of her poufy pink dress. And in a little glass dish on top of that dresser, there are dozens of shiny hair clips, exactly like the ones Emily and Sadie use.

"What does Emily think of the name Runa?" I ask.

"That it's sort of weird but sort of cool, but maybe I should go by my middle name someday."

"Oh."

Runa's middle name is Hope, which is a nice word and a nice name too, I guess, but it isn't *her* name.

I move from the bed to the floor, and Runa shifts to make room for me next to her. We like a particular patch of rug in Runa's room: the corner by the bed so we can lean against it and be close to each other and not be seen when Runa's parents open the door to check in on us. It's like a hiding place that isn't a hiding place, and I'm relieved that, at least, hasn't changed. We still fit perfectly right here.

The Tale of Dragons True

Denny, age 7

A queen's job is to teach the princess how to be.

They travel to faraway kingdoms.

She teaches her to braid her hair.

They throw parties together, with delicate crystal plates and twenty-two-layer cakes and pony rides in the royal yard.

The queen teaches the princess to punish mean creatures. Witches with bad curses. Fairies causing mischief. Dragons in bad moods.

There is one witch in Sorrowfeld. She lives on the Lake of Leer.

Chapter 3

Denny Greene
Seven Days Before the Swap

Mom's got a slice of toast with peanut butter and the same tired look on her face she's had for months. In the mornings, her eyes are glassy and she's distracted and antsy, like she's waiting for me to leave her alone. But when I talk to her, she responds, at least. She'll sign off on a field trip or remind me to wear rain boots. At night she mostly shuts herself in her room, and we can't see her, but we can feel the force of her from behind the door—heavy and sad and scary.

And then there are the other days. They don't come often, but enough. Something makes her angry, and her voice is scratchy and mean. She tells me I hate her on those days, and maybe I do, but not the way she thinks.

I hate the closed door and shaking hands and this sickly-sweet smell that comes off her. I hate the space between the mom I used to have and the one she's turned into over the last year.

On Saturday mornings, we used to make surprise toast for each other. I'd make her mashed banana and honey. She'd give me cream cheese with sprinkles. I'd melt cheese on hers. She'd melt chocolate on mine.

Mom's toast today looks wrong. The peanut butter is unevenly spread, the crust is burnt, and she's not even eating it.

I don't have toast. I poured myself a bowl of cereal. Honestly, I don't really eat toast for breakfast anymore. I don't like how it makes me feel.

"So, my party is in a week," I say. "I guess, um, Runa and I mostly planned it. Unless you had something you wanted to do? Or any ideas?"

Mom always has ideas. Decorations or cool games that I'd never think of or ridiculous themed food that is somehow funny and beautiful and delicious all at once. For a moment, I let myself hope that she'll have an idea for this birthday too, my twelfth. I'd sort of like to stay eleven, but the old version of Mom could make me excited to celebrate twelve. She'd think of something spectacular and strange to make it special.

Maybe old Mom is somewhere under this new one,

with her uneaten toast and gruff voice and uneven way of walking.

Maybe old Mom is hiding out with old Runa, and maybe, maybe I can find them both, and then I can stay old Denny.

"It's too early in the morning to talk about this kind of thing," Mom says. Her voice is flat, tense. "Ask your dad, okay?" She sounds the way I do when my feelings get hurt by something Sadie has said to me and someone notices and asks if I'm okay, and I'm not okay but if I say that I'll cry, so I say something else instead. Her shaking hands pick up the toast, then put it back down.

Those same hands used to sew outfits for my stuffed animals, paint landscapes from our back porch, grip bike handles on long rides to the beach. Now they mostly grip heavy thermoses filled with not-coffee and pull the covers over her head and shut the door.

And shake and shake and shake.

"Maybe we could talk about it tomorrow or something?" I ask. I try to make my voice sound nice, so nice that she can't get mad at it, so nice that she feels better and lifts her head and looks right at me and smiles. I can picture Mom holding a blue birthday cake with eleven candles on it, grinning from ear to ear, singing the silly version of "Happy Birthday," about smelling like a monkey, which always cracked her up. I remember the banner she made and decorated in glitter for my tenth birthday, and the way she looked on roller skates at my ninth, like she was some kind of Olympic roller skater.

It feels like I should be able to connect the dots from that person to this one and bring them together again. Like if Mom could just remember the way it used to be, she'd of course want to be that way again.

But she can't remember.

Over the years, Mom and Dad have tried to explain alcoholism to me a lot, and I get it—it has to do with drinking and not knowing how to stop and being addicted and it's a disease just like any other disease. That all makes sense, sort of, but what doesn't make sense is that for a long, long time—most of my life—Mom wasn't sick like this. For a long time, before I was born, Mom *had* been sick, then she got pregnant with me and she got better, like magic. Sober. And she was magically sober almost my whole life.

It's a part of the story that used to make me feel shiny and proud—that Mom and I have such a special thing going that she stopped being sick, that my arrival made everyone happy and new. Now that part of the story makes me feel something else, something cramped and hot. Whatever special thing Mom and I had, it wasn't enough.

I wasn't enough.

Because a little over a year ago, she got sick again. Right around the time she lost her job teaching art at the college in town. She got sad. Then mad. Then so tired she didn't get out of bed. Then she started drinking, even though my whole life she'd said she was so glad she'd stopped.

It took a while to figure out that she'd started drinking again. At first everything just felt . . . tilted. Tilted and a little bit scary in a way I couldn't put my finger on. I asked and asked and asked why Mom seemed tired, why Mom didn't want to talk to me, why Mom was mad at me, why why why why why why.

They didn't like me asking why.

But it's a good thing I did, because I asked so many times one night that even though Dad mostly likes to just tell me not to worry instead of actually doing anything, this night he couldn't take all my questions anymore, so he marched downstairs to tell Mom to explain to me because he was tired of trying to explain what she was feeling, and instead of Mom sleeping, she was sitting in their window seat, pouring a glass of wine into her thermos.

I used to love that window seat.

It's stained now, though, from when she threw the thermos on the ground because she was so mad we'd come in. It's stained, and I don't want to sit in it again, anyway. I hate that window seat now.

Meanwhile, Dad keeps saying she got better before so she will again, and I guess that must be true, but I don't know why it's taking so long or what I can do to speed it up. But I keep trying to lead her there, like if I bring her enough memories of the person she used to be, she'll remember how to be that person again.

"I just thought, you usually like birthday parties, so maybe you'd want—" I start, saying it as softly as I can, even though underneath the softness is all the wanting and worry in the world.

"I'm doing my best," Mom interrupts. Her face is pinched, her hair flat. She doesn't wear her favorite jeans anymore, doesn't use her collection of headbands she's known for. The shape of her face seems different even. Rounder. Redder. Sadder.

"I wasn't trying to make you—"

"I can't start the day this way, Denny. I just can't."

I want to ask which way—talking to me? Eating toast? Thinking about birthdays? But I think one of the ways she means is me asking her questions, so I hold it back.

Maybe being quiet will help.

Maybe answering my own questions will help.

Maybe tiptoeing to my room to worry about my birthday party alone will help.

I just know Dad keeps saying we can help her, so I have to figure out what that means.

I did it before, just by being born. So surely I can do it again.

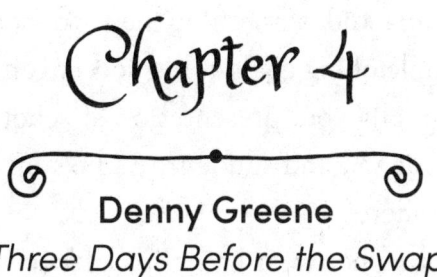

Chapter 4

Denny Greene
Three Days Before the Swap

Runa hands me a yellow hair clip before lunch. It feels important.

We used to bring each other little treasures all the time, but not lately. I have a list in my head of what has changed and what has not changed, because I want to make sure I can see it clearly. Not bringing each other sea glass or comic books or perfect pine cones is one of the things that has definitely changed.

Other things haven't. I still know Runa's mom's middle name, I was invited to her family's Fourth of July party, and she's told me all about what she really thinks of the boy everyone thinks is cute.

And we still have Sorrowfeld. And how she knows when I do and do not want to talk about my mom. And that list I made for her once, of everything special about her, when she was feeling upset that Sadie didn't invite her to her birthday party.

Then Runa did something new to her hair and scored a couple of big goals at her soccer games and her mom did a really cool presentation at school on being a jewelry designer, and suddenly Sadie started inviting Runa everywhere.

And making her wear hair clips and a certain brand of jeans and a billion friendship bracelets around her wrists.

The list of what has stayed the same is always colliding with the list of what has changed.

"What's this for?" I ask. I have not been instructed, yet, to wear special jeans and clips in my hair. I'm not sure I want to be asked. But I hold the clip like it's fragile—special—anyway.

"For luck," she whispers.

At first, I think she means luck for lunch. It would make sense. Lately lunch is the sort of place I need luck. Runa wants to sit with Emily and Sadie, and they let me sit there too, but it feels different than the corner table Runa and I used to sit at. Sometimes we'd be alone there, sometimes a friend would join us—kids from other grades or from after-school theater, or who we've known forever in the neighborhood. I miss the table—the way it wobbled, how it was underneath a window that was always cracked open the tiniest bit, how you could see the whole cafeteria from there, see everyone eating and chatting and just being. I always liked watching.

Then I think maybe the lucky clip is for our birthday party this weekend. It's starting to feel like something I need luck for—twenty kids I'm not really friends with coming over to our house, to have a party I don't even really understand.

"Luck?" I ask.

"They announced auditions," Runa says. "End of next week." She points at a poster on the cafeteria door.

The Wizard of Oz

Follow the Yellow Brick Road to the auditorium Monday, February 23. Bring your brain, heart, courage, and a short song. Sides will be provided.

"Yellow Brick Road, yellow clip," Runa says. "You'll look great."

I don't really like wearing accessories. I have short

honey-colored hair and thick bangs, and I don't normally do much of anything but brush it out and let it be. Still, it's nice of Runa to want to include me, and even nicer that she knows how much I want to be in the show. I put the clip in my hair. Runa scrunches up her mouth like it doesn't look the way she imagined it would, but she doesn't try to fix it before we walk over to our new, bustling table.

"Cute clip." Emily greets me, but it could be sarcastic. It's always hard to tell with Emily, who says almost everything with a little bit of a bite.

"You guys see the poster?" Sadie asks instead of saying hello. Everyone knows Sadie is the best singer in the grade. She almost always gets a solo at the holiday concert, and when we sing "Happy Birthday" to anyone in class, she does a fancy harmony. "I've been practicing 'Over the Rainbow.' It's not an easy song, you know? But Dorothy is my dream role."

"It's Denny's dream role, too," Runa says. For a moment I'm just relieved she called me Denny, and she's not seriously expecting me to go by Auden. Then the relief passes, and I turn the color of one of the tomatoes Mom used to pick from the garden, back when she was still gardening.

"Denny doesn't sing," Sadie says, as if she can tell just by looking at me.

For a moment, Runa looks uncertain, but I see her

shake her head the tiniest bit before she puts back her shoulders the way she does when she's telling her mom why it's only fair that we get to have two sleepovers on the weekend instead of just one.

"She actually has a really pretty voice," Runa says. "She's just shy."

"I might not even audition," I say, partly because it's true and partly because I want Runa to stop talking about me like I'm not right here. Everything she knows about me seems to just be slipping out, and some of it is nice—like that she thinks my voice is pretty—but all of it is stuff that I thought was only between us.

"Of course you're auditioning," Runa says, barely even looking at me and the way my face won't stop being red and my armpits won't stop being damp and my whole body is trying to turn in on itself, the way certain blooms close up at night—crocuses and tulips and poppies. All the flowers Mom most loved to grow. Now the garden out back is messy, covered in weeds. I'm starting to forget the way Mom looked in her gardening gloves, her way-too-big sun hat shading her face.

"Do you act?" Sadie asks, interrupting those thoughts. Her nose is wrinkled like even the idea of it is horrifying.

I shrug. I try to give Runa a look that says this conversation needs to end, but she ignores it. There's some way I'm supposed to be, but she forgot to tell me what it is, and I'm not sure I want to be that way. She straightens out a few of her hair clips.

"Denny loves acting," she says. "Just like you, Sadie!" Her voice is extra cheery, but underneath all that cheer is a hum of worry.

"I guess I sort of want to," I say.

The truth is that I spend entire Saturdays lying on my back blasting Broadway soundtracks, imagining myself as Maria in *The Sound of Music* and Elphaba in *Wicked* and Annie in *Annie* and lately, for hours and hours and hours on end, Dorothy in *The Wizard of Oz*. I can see myself with the pigtails, the blue-and-white dress, the basket over my arm. I love how Dorothy goes from her boring home in Kansas, where she can't help much of anything, to the golden-roaded world of Oz, where she is powerful and beloved and maybe even magical. Where everyone believes she is someone special, someone to be adored or maybe feared, but definitely noticed. I love how she makes unexpected friends along the way, and I love most of all that she is dreamy and wanting and brave and kind.

"Well, my dad says you have to more than want it. You have to dedicate your whole self to the things you care about. Talent only goes so far, you know," Sadie says, as if she's reading from a manual her father wrote.

I almost feel bad for her. We all know Sadie's dad. He sits in the front row at every school concert, every parents' day, with his arms crossed and his mouth frowning, waiting to be impressed. I wonder if he ever has been.

"Oh wait. I remember now," Sadie goes on, lighting up a little. "The talent show—you tried to sing, right? And couldn't?" Her voice is louder than it needs to be, and people are listening in, the way they always do when Sadie's decided she needs to be heard.

"Sadie. Come on," Runa says. Runa reminds me of the picture of the princess turning into the dragon on her wall. She is half old Runa and half new Runa.

"I mean, we were all at the talent show, it's not a secret," Sadie says. People at nearby tables raise their eyebrows, grimace, stop a laugh before it comes out.

There's a warm rush of shame that flies through me. Sweat floods my neck, my knees, my lower back. I'd hoped they'd forgotten. I'd hoped it was one of those moments that was bigger for me than for everyone else, like how I always remember the night there was a thunderstorm so loud it woke me up or exactly which pies Dad made for Thanksgiving dinner last year when Mom didn't come out of her room, even though when I bring up thunderstorms and pies, no one else seems to have the same almost-touchable memories.

I'd hoped my talent show failure was a thunderstorm in July or a caramel-pumpkin-walnut pie.

"Maybe you shouldn't waste the director's time,"

Sadie says. She's on a roll, getting louder and more animated the more she notices people listening in. "It would be weird to run off the stage again." Her voice is acting like this is a nice thing to say. The sound is sweet. But the words are all bite.

A new girl whose name I don't know makes eye contact with me, tilts her head, and mouths, *Are you okay?* She has a headband with cat ears and a red beaded necklace and braces and a shirt with a fairy on it.

I nod that I'm okay, but I'm not and she can probably tell because she doesn't stop watching, like she might come save me if it gets any worse.

"Leave her alone," Emily says, maybe noticing how strange this conversation is, how tense Sadie looks, and how I am trying to lose myself in a Tupperware container of pasta salad.

Or maybe Emily's just bored of talking about it. She rolls her eyes.

"I'm just saying, not everyone's cut out to be an actress," Sadie insists.

When I first started practicing to audition for the play, Runa said acting was weird, because it was like lying with permission. "But I guess you have permission to lie these days," she'd gone on. "Because of your mom."

Runa was always saying things out loud that no one

else ever would. I could have pretended to not know what she was talking about, but I did know. In the last year or so, it has all become a lie—the pretty house and my brushed hair and the airy, easy way I have to answer when someone asks me how my parents are. *Good, good. My mom's been busy, that's why you haven't seen her at stuff lately. She's good. She's just getting over the flu. But she's great, she was just here, you must have just missed her.*

Mom got sick again, and without telling me exactly, my parents gave me permission to lie.

So I don't exactly agree that I'm not cut out to be an actress. I'm acting all the time.

And if I really were Dorothy, I'd calmly tell her how wrong she is. I'd explain that just because I seem quiet doesn't mean I'm not talented, doesn't mean I'm too scared to get up onstage. I'd tell her she can forget about last time; this time will be different. If I were Dorothy, I'd walk right away from this table to sit with the new girl with the cat ears and the ruby-red necklace, and Runa would probably follow me.

But I'm Denny, not Dorothy. So I don't say anything at all.

And, I realize with a hitch of hurt so big I could get lost in it, neither does Runa.

The Tale of Dragons True

Denny, age 11

You'd think, just by looking at it, that Sorrowfeld is a safe and beautiful kingdom. The castle is so pretty, the moat sparkles. The royal yard is full of daffodils, roses, sunflowers. There are royal balls almost daily.

But Sorrowfeld is not the kingdom you think it is.

Hidden in the kingdom there are witches. Dragons.

And the feeling that it all might get destroyed.

Smoke in the sky. The way a witch sounds when she's laughing. The shaky feeling of things not being as they seem. Sorrowfeld is in trouble. Maybe the princess will save it. Maybe the dragons will.

Someone has to.

Chapter 5

Denny Greene
Two Hours Before the Swap

For the first time ever, the morning of our birthday party comes too quickly. There are streamers to hang and snacks to put into bowls and the sick feeling in my stomach to try to calm. Runa keeps checking her brand-new birthday present phone to make sure everyone important is still coming.

I bought Runa a journal of her own for her birthday, and I left it in the shed, where we always leave each other gifts. I tried to find one that was sophisticated, the sort of thing she can make party-planning notes in, a place she can, I don't know, write down what outfits Sadie thinks are cool or how she's supposed to do her hair every day of the week so she can fit in. At least that way, she'll stop writing about that awful world in the book meant only for our magical one.

Dad's trying extra hard to seem happy, which is very different than Dad actually *being* happy, but I get the feeling Dad doesn't think I notice the difference. He's blowing up balloons and filling a cooler with ice and cans of soda. Mom is where Mom always is—in the bedroom.

"She'll come down soon," he says. "She loves birthday parties. She was talking about it yesterday, even. How much this will cheer her up."

Dad sort of blushes, like he knows he's exaggerating whatever hum or tight smile or one-word answer Mom gave him.

I hate when Dad talks about Mom's illness like it is just a case of the blues. I hate when he tries to erase the clang of bottles in our recycling, the stringiness of her hair when she doesn't shower, that she threw her hair dryer onto the ground one time when I asked her for help with my homework.

But maybe I'm not much better, because I don't tell Runa everything either.

She doesn't know about the smell the hair dryer made, broken like that. A melty-plastic, nothing-makes-sense, everything-is-falling-apart sort of smell.

I suspect Runa might not want to be here at all, but our birthday party is always at my house, and the one time Runa asked if it was a good idea to have it here this year, I said yes it was a good idea, not because it was true, but because I really, really wanted it to be true.

Runa had looked at me like she was waiting for me to correct myself, but I didn't, and she didn't, and so here we are, both of us wishing we could go back to that day and say what is obvious—that my mom hasn't even come to school pickup in months, so she is definitely not in a place to be hosting a birthday party.

Runa doesn't say that, though. Instead, she can't stop talking about the decorations. Streamers and balloons are for little kids, the music Dad put on is for little kids, and even I, in a purple dress and mustard-yellow tights and a birthday crown because I always make us birthday crowns, am like a little kid.

"We're turning *twelve*," Runa says to Dad, who has mounted Pin the Tail on the Dragon onto our kitchen wall.

"Twelve-year-olds still get to have fun," Dad says with a wink. "Denny, can you go grab your mom? I know she won't want to miss everyone arriving."

"Are you sure?" I ask this question a lot about Mom. It's a sort of code we use. *Are you sure?* means *Is Mom actually okay enough to handle this?*

"It's your birthday," Dad says. He whispers it like it's a secret, like it's our last chance, like it's everything, and maybe it is. "She would never miss your birthday."

I can't tell if it's the truth or just the thing we want to be true.

I don't know what will happen if it turns out to be not true at all.

Not very long ago, I would have been sure of so much between Mom and me. On my birthday, she would have told the story of the day she found out she was having me, and how it changed everything, how I changed everything, fixed what had been hurting her, made the world sunnier and sweeter and just plain better.

I don't know how to make the world feel that way for her again. I don't know why the magic was so easy to break apart.

I can't argue with Dad or explain any of this, because he's acting clueless and overly smiley, so I amble upstairs and find Mom in bed, of course, and she looks lost, like maybe she's forgotten that today exists. Was it really only a year ago that we were talking through all the possible themes for my eleventh birthday? *Underwater My Little Ponies Extravaganza* and *Art and Popsicles and Tutus* and *Chocolate Dragon Scavenger Hunt*.

Without Mom taking the lead, there's no theme this year, although if I had to pick one, it would be *Trying to Be Popular While Eating Cake and Playing Twister*.

"Mom?" I try. "The party's starting. Runa's here."

"Okay," she says. It sounds like it takes a lot of effort for her to say even just that, so I shift my body ever so slightly out of the room.

"Dad thought you might want to join."

"I can't join. You know I can't join." She's quiet and half here. It's one of three ways she is, lately, and Dad seems to know exactly what each of them means. There's weepy and wild. There's mean and confused. There's flat quiet and not quite here.

I can't ever decide which one is worst. Whatever one she's in is the one that's worst, I guess.

We should have had the party at Runa's house. We should have not had a party at all, maybe. A feeling I am getting used to twists itself from my stomach to my throat. It's either fear or sadness or dread or maybe all three, I'm not sure.

"Okay," I say. "So I'll—okay. Good night?" It's noon.

"Night," Mom mutters back, and maybe she says, "Happy birthday," or maybe I just am hoping I'm hearing it in between mumbles.

It's not night. She should not be in bed. I don't care how many times Dad explains the disease of alcoholism and words like *relapse* and *sobriety* and *depression*, I can't seem to make sense of the way things are.

Some mornings, I get a glimpse of old Mom, and

it feels like maybe things will be okay again, and then the day goes on and she yells at me for something I don't even know is wrong, like asking for a ride to the library or wondering if we could go out for burgers, and then before the sun goes down, she's in bed and Dad's pacing and making up excuses and asking if I'm okay a hundred times, even though he knows I'm not.

I shut the door behind me.

And somehow when I get downstairs, my birthday party is filled with people that Runa is hugging and squealing with but who barely even wave in my direction.

I pull at my tights. I unbutton and rebutton the top of my dress. My fingers play piano on my hips, a tune that is also, probably, all wrong.

"She coming?" Dad asks, before I can make it over to Runa's side, which is the only place I really want to be.

"No."

"Did you try?" Dad's eyes are so sad, his shoulders are so drooped, I can tell he thought Mom would become Mom again on my birthday, like Cinderella shifting back into herself at the stroke of midnight. My birthday was supposed to fix her.

"I can try again," I say. "Maybe I didn't say the right thing."

"I'm sure you did your best," Dad says, the forced

cheeriness in his tone even sadder than just regular sadness. My best is obviously not good enough, not even close, and we both just stand there, wondering why I'm not enough anymore.

I catch Runa looking at me, looking around at the party, looking up the stairs, then looking at me again, and I'm pretty sure she's thinking the same.

Three more girls arrive. They hug Runa, hand over presents, and look around the living room. I'm not sure what they're looking for, but I can tell that what *is* here doesn't measure up. There are cupcakes and popcorn and miniature SunButter sandwiches and Pin the Tail on the Dragon, and Twister, and a few tables with board games set up, and not much else. Other kids do pool parties or sleepover parties or makeover parties, but I've never needed any of that. I always just had Mom's brand of magic and Runa by my side.

Sadie comes over to me while I'm trying to think of something cool and normal to say to Runa that could paper over the awkwardness of everything.

"So, like, what are we doing for fun?" Sadie asks.

"Um, this?" I say.

"Oh. Right. Games and stuff. Cute."

"Yeah, I guess that's what a birthday party is, right?"

I have to imagine that for some people words come

out without thinking, without worrying, and then once they're out they just stay there, fitting right in with the couches and teacups and wallpaper. But words aren't like that for me. They're hard to find, first of all, and whenever I do come across some and am brave enough to actually say them, they arrive all wrong. They are messy and awkward and just plain bad. Like a pile of bricks dropped in a crystal palace. Like a princess dress at a cool girl's birthday party.

"It reminds me of my eighth birthday party," Sadie says, smiling through the meanness.

"It wasn't Runa's idea," I say, because at least she should be saved from whatever they're all thinking about us now.

"Obviously." Sadie's mouth moves like it's itching, like she's eaten something salty or spicy or a little too hot. "Runa's cool."

"Oh," I say. "Right."

Sadie turns away, and it's not like she said, exactly, that I'm *not* cool, but she sort of did, I think.

I look around for Runa, because I have to tell someone what Sadie said, and like magic, she's next to me. She looks taller than she did yesterday, her hair seems longer too, and fluffier, maybe. I think she's wearing another lipstick. And maybe blush. And definitely eyeshadow, a sparkly lavender kind. I didn't know we were supposed to wear makeup to the party, but I should have guessed. I didn't know we were supposed to be making our hair fluffier. I didn't know that people don't like Twister.

"Your friends don't think I'm cool," I say. With Runa, I find words more easily, but they're always the really direct kind. That used to be okay, but lately I wish I could find fancier, more roundabout ways to talk to her.

"They don't think the *party* is cool," Runa whispers, "because it isn't."

I think maybe she's saying it to be mean, but when I look at her really closely, I see her face is flushed not just from pink blush, and her eyes are watery, like they want to cry.

"You don't even try, Denny. This is important to me. Let's do it together. They said you can be friends with us too. I swear. I told them how funny you are and how good at singing and that you could totally fit in with us. And you can! If you just, like, *try*. I don't want to do this without you. But, you know."

She doesn't finish the sentence, but I think she means to say she doesn't want to do this without me—but she will if she has to.

My dress feels itchy. My shoes feel tight. Dad turns some music on, and I can tell from the way Emily's shoulders shift forward that it is the wrong type of music. "I wanted it to just be us and a couple friends and pizza and a movie or something," I say. I feel like crying too. "Like always. With you and me staying up late after in the shed with *The Tale of Dragons True* and—"

"That's what babies do," Runa says. She says it loud enough for a few people to hear, and they do. Sadie smirks. Emily laughs.

"I thought that's what *we* do," I say. My voice feels shallow. My heart hiccups. Runa had said she thought it might be nice to be a dragon, but I didn't know she really meant it. I didn't know she might become one right here and now, in the middle of our birthday party, destroying all the things that remind her of who we are, who we've always been.

"We're *twelve*," Runa says for the second time. It means something to her that it doesn't mean to me. She's been writing it into our Sorrowfeld stories too. Insisting that princesses come into their powers at twelve, that everything changes at twelve, that they become more important, more grown-up, more special.

"Runa?" It's Sadie again, her voice jabbing and mean. "My mom said she could drive us to go bowling. It's not, like, amazing or anything, but it's better than this."

Runa doesn't like bowling. It's one of a hundred things I know about her. That she doesn't like bowling. That she thinks the best way to eat eggs is on top of pancakes. That she got a C-minus in English last year. That she knows how to draw a dragon face that looks both sad and scary. That her mom and dad sing her a lullaby before bed at night like they did when she was a baby, because it helps her sleep.

"I love bowling," Runa says. "Bowling is perfect."

The Tale of Dragons True

Runa, age 11

True princesses need to reckon with their pasts, let go of their childish ways.

A true princess is in charge of her kingdom. She is now a royal, meant to be listened to, respected, beloved.

Only a true princess can defeat a dragon. She knows in her heart how to do it.

No one else can help her.

A true princess is not a child anymore.

A true princess is twelve. Everything changes at twelve.

Chapter 6

Denny Greene
The Swap

"You can come," Runa says, seeing my face respond to the idea that she's going to leave our birthday party when it's barely even begun.

"I can't come," I say, my hands sweating, tingling, my neck tight, tense. "How could I come? My dad is throwing us *this* party, here, right now. And you invited all these kids. Are you telling them all to just go bowling instead? My dad's feelings would be really—"

I hate the way my voice sounds. Desperate.

But Runa doesn't notice the way my toes are curling or how my words are all wavy and wild. She's looking at one thing only—the stairs. Mom's coming down them, but she seems wobbly and on her face is an expression that is trying to be a smile. Everything in my body wants to push her back up the stairs, shove everything that's happening somewhere else.

"See, I'm at the party," Mom says. "Okay? I'm here."

She is half sad and half mad, and I want to leave my own body.

"Hey, Mom, you want cake or something maybe?" I ask, trying to cover it up with normalness. Besides, Mom loves cake. Sometimes she used to make it at night, the kind from the box, after I went to bed, and in the morning there would be cake for breakfast. My brain feels like it's splitting in half, trying to make sense of the mom who surprised me with cake for breakfast and this person, wobbly and not really smiling, who I guess is my mom too, even though that still feels impossible.

"Cake is a great idea," Dad says, but anyone can see that Mom isn't about to pull it together to become some magical birthday-loving being. She's in her pajamas and pushing her hair back like that might make her look normal.

Then she seems to give up and sits down on the stairs, too tired from the effort of whatever she's just done. She puts her head in her hands and snaps at Dad to leave her alone.

"I told you I'm *tired*," she says, her voice in a knot. "I told you I wasn't able to come, and you just all pushed and pushed, and now— I'm not hungry. Cake is too— I can't eat cake."

She looks up and sees me, Runa, the other kids. A sob escapes, the kind that sounds like something heavy dropping to the ground, and she hides her face in her hands. "I'm sorry," she says. Then she says it three more times.

I wish I could cover it all up, or at least understand the journey Mom takes from one feeling to another. I can't seem to keep up with what's wrong or why it's wrong or how she wants me to fix it, like a dot-connecting activity book that someone scribbled all over, so you can't see the image that's supposed to come into focus when all the lines are drawn correctly.

I'm so hot I can barely breathe. It is all wrong, wrong, wrong. I have a nice, normal mom who paints her nails pink every Saturday, who knows my friends' names and makes silly jokes in a silly voice. I have a mom who walks down the stairs on her own, who is pretty good at face painting and salsa dancing, who would never, never do this.

I cross my arms around my middle to hold in the way it feels, and I close my mouth tight.

Runa takes a step away from Mom and Dad and the stairs, but that is also a step away from me. I lean toward her like I might pull her back to me, but I don't. I can't.

"So yeah. Bowling," Sadie says, raising her eyebrows and looking around the room for agreement.

"You should come," Runa says again, which I guess is also her saying that she's leaving, that they're all leaving, that our birthday is over before it even began. I can tell she doesn't really mean it. The thing happening in my family is too big, too impossible. I don't want to be around me either, really.

I don't know how to be Denny, whose mom is falling apart on the stairs in front of everyone, and also Denny, cool fifth grader with friends and bowling shoes. I only get to be one. And I don't get to choose.

I shake my head, and Runa is relieved enough to remember to hug me and whisper that it will be okay.

"Save me a slice of cake," she says. "I'll try to come over later. After. We can still have a sleepover." She looks at Mom and Dad again. "Or bring the cake to my place? We can stay at my place tonight. Okay? I'll tell my mom. She can pick you up."

I nod, but I know it won't happen. I live here, in this world, and Runa lives out there, where things are still okay, where things make sense.

Dad sits down next to Mom and rubs her back. Kids get their jackets, their backpacks. Everyone with phones starts tapping away at them, telling parents the new plan, securing rides, getting out of here.

Dad doesn't seem to notice the room emptying out. He's focused on Mom and the pace of her breath—fast—and the swimminess of her eyes. A few kids try to say thank you to him, but their voices barely lift out of their throats, and most of them just give up and head out to our lawn. Dad hung a piñata up out there—a dragon one, of course—and I watch through the window as kids take swings at it. They're laughing, passing a stick around, spinning each other with eyes closed to make it more of a challenge, and even Runa is smiling. A minute ago, she said it was babyish and wrong, but they're all having fun, so I don't know what's true.

"Over the Rainbow" comes on the playlist Dad had set up for the party, and it's not exactly a party song, but he knows it's the one I have to nail at the audition tomorrow, now more than ever. I love the song, but right now I can't listen to it. The way Judy Garland sings it—so filled with the wanting of things to be different—is too close to this exact moment. Dad is whispering something to Mom, and cars are starting to arrive outside, and my birthday cake is just sitting there, and I know with absolute certainty that it is never going to get eaten, not even one little bite, and finally I fly out of the room, out of the house, to the garden shed.

Right away, it's better in the shed than it could ever be out there. Dragons. Broadway posters. And *The Tale of Dragons True* is still open to the party-planning page, which I think I should rip out of the book, maybe, since it doesn't belong there, it never belonged there.

On top of the book there is a present wrapped in shiny purple paper. *To Denny love Runa*, says a card taped to the top, in Runa's familiar handwriting. I surge with a sort of relief that something has remained the same. The book I bought her is gone, so she must have taken it and left this gift for me. We're still us. Or we're not, but we still have this.

I open the gift, and I'm worried that there's something inside that's meant to tell me who I need to be now. Shimmery lip gloss or more hair clips or a tiny, too-tight T-shirt or, I don't know, a guidebook on how to be twelve, how to be cool, how to stop being a kid and start being whatever the next thing is.

But instead what's inside is a promise that Runa is still, at least in some small way, mine. Her gift to me is a small, heavy mirror, a circle made up of four brass dragons, each one reaching for the next, wings jutting out, mouths open, the carving of them so detailed you can practically hear their wings flapping, their fiery breath bursting. The mirror itself is foggy and scratched—I can only really see the outline of me in it—the color of my hair, the shape of my face, not any of my precise details.

It is a mirror that belongs in Sorrowfeld, a thing that looks like it was made exactly for our invented kingdom.

It's perfect.

I sit on the ground and look at the posters and open our little treasure box and pick up two of the clay dragons that Runa and I made—one is red-striped, and one has a twisted neck and spikes on its back and this look on its face like it's going to survive, no matter what.

There's nothing much to do in the shed without Runa. I wonder what she's up to—bowling, I guess, and talking about who looks cute and maybe trying on Emily's makeup that she carries in a shiny silver purse everywhere she goes, or maybe looking at Sadie's phone, since her parents let her have social media. I bet they're laughing at videos. I bet they're convincing Runa to dye her hair blond or to wear more plaid or to join the field hockey team.

I'm not jealous of Runa for being included. I don't want to play field hockey or wear the right earrings or try to put on eye shadow or be a teenager already. I don't want a body in a different shape or my period or everyone to ask who I have a crush on and then make a big huge deal out of it.

I want to think about dragons.

I want to make kingdoms out of thin air.

I want Mom to check on me in the shed—her special knockity-knock-knock at the window, her offer to make me a hot chocolate, to go on a walk with me.

I want that, all of it: Runa and dragons and belting "Tomorrow" and my mom joining in, singing along, her voice always surprising me with its depth, its prettiness. I want it because I used to have it. A special magic that made our family beautiful. A shimmery bond with Mom that was easy. It used to be mine.

I hear Runa's voice in my head—we're supposed to do something new now. And I want that too, I guess, just not in the same way she does.

I want to wear Dorothy's blue dress and ruby-red shoes and go on a quest and feel all her feelings instead of mine and see what it's like to be on a stage with everyone watching, wondering if you can hit the high notes.

And I can. I can hit them. I can't be cool like Sadie or as sophisticated as Emily, but I can hit all the notes and feel all the feelings, and if I'm brave, maybe I will get to spend time being Dorothy instead of Denny.

It is so much wanting. Wanting something that used to be and wanting something that might become and wanting, even, to want what Runa wants. Wanting to not be wanting all alone.

I start to sing "Over the Rainbow," my voice hitching a little from the way the day is all wrong but the words are all right. I watch the fuzzy version of me in the mirror. I like how the glass is so distorted I could be anyone. I get lost in the song and in the mirror me. I finish singing and it feels almost like I can face the world again. I take a deep breath and put down the mirror.

But my world isn't there.

I am somewhere else.

At the base of an enormous lilac-stoned castle. It is tall and turreted, and the air smells a little like fire but not the charcoal-and-burgers kind. There is a noise in the distance but it is not the honking of horns, the occasional snippet of blasted-radio music. It sounds like the flapping of wings. It sounds like something fast approaching; it sounds like the end of something.

Or maybe the beginning.

Chapter 7

Princess Auden
Three Hours Before the Swap

Every year I do not want a party, and every year a party gets thrown for me anyway. It is not true, really, what I've heard townspeople mumble—that princesses get whatever they want. In many ways, princesses get what everyone else wants, and what everyone else wants is a royal birthday party.

Even though they know what happens at my birthday parties.

"We should do five cakes," Lady Genevive says. "Or ten!" She is not really a lady—just an eleven-year-old girl like me, except she's allowed to stay a kid and I'm about to become something else, I suppose.

"Lady Genevive. Please." I'm more nervous about this year than all the others combined. This year I'm expected to save the kingdom. Maybe that sounds like a party to everyone else, but it sounds truly awful to me.

"It's your birthday, Princess Auden. We must celebrate." Lady Genevive makes notes in the royal ledger. She is buzzing with hope, with excitement. They all are. The whole kingdom has felt sparkly and alive as we've gotten closer to my party.

"Maybe they won't come if we don't celebrate," I say. There's nothing in *The Tale of Dragons True* that says this is a possibility, but there is also nothing in the book that says dragons visit on birthdays. We just know they visit on mine.

The book changes, and lately it's been changing quite a lot. There are pages and pages now on dragons and how we should feel bad for them, how they used to be human. Lady Genevive's father, Duke Verden, says this is to be ignored. Dragons are not humans. That's absurd. We've always believed dragons are born from golden eggs. This new wrinkle is the witch trying to trick us. The enchanted text is important, but it's open to interpretation. And Duke Verden is who interprets it.

I wish he had an interpretation for why dragons fly in the skies around the castle every year on my birthday, knocking stones from the castle walls, ripping old trees right from the ground. Year after year I run to my room and hide under the covers. Every year Duke Verden reminds me this is unbecoming of a princess.

"My father says it is important to go on with traditions even in the face of danger," Lady Genevive says. I don't say that it's easy for him to make declarations like that, because no one is expecting *him* to fight dragons. Duke Verden has been in charge for a long time, but soon I will be of age.

In the last year, *The Tale of Dragons True* has started insisting that princesses become true princesses at age twelve. We ignored it at first, the way we ignore some of the little shifts and shake-ups in the enchanted text. Magic is fickle, after all. But the text is insistent. *Twelve, twelve, twelve*, it keeps saying. *Everything changes at twelve.*

The rest of the kingdom has gotten excited about this new bit of information. It means there's a solution. They're ready to celebrate the dawn of a new, safer era in Sorrowfeld. An era without dragons. An era that they all seem to think starts today.

I do not know how to explain that I cannot possibly be the solution to this problem. I am certain I am not the princess they want me to be.

I don't respond to Lady Genevive, who is always parroting what her father says. Duke Verden is in charge for just a few more hours. I have done what he's asked. Trained in all the ways one might defeat a dragon—swords and fire throwing and mixing potions and throwing rocks. I have learned to yell and hide and run fast, since that might dizzy them, confuse them, disorient them enough for them to fall apart. No one knows how a dragon is defeated, so I've been taught everything Duke Verden can think of. He also says I'll know what to do when the time comes, that maybe those skills will help or maybe there is some other way to defeat a dragon that will be revealed.

The details about dragons in *The Tale of Dragons True* are patchy and shifting, passages vanishing from the book, then reappearing, written in slightly different words. There are missing pages, blurry pages, and pages you think you read once, but can't seem to find ever again. I'd never say it out loud, but I hate the text. It never said that my family would be taken by dragons, so how much does it really know, anyway?

I have no idea how Duke Verden decides which pieces are to be believed, like the ones that say I can solve everything, and which are to be dismissed.

But Duke Verden is a scholar of *The Tale of Dragons True*. He spends all his time studying it and interpreting it for the rest of us. So I suppose he should be trusted.

He was put in charge of me when I was practically a baby, when I had no one at all. He's all I have.

Even if he makes me do this cursed party every year.

"When I am a real princess, I'll do away with birthday parties," I say. Then I remember that that day is today. In a few hours, I will be a real princess. I wiggle my fingers, blink my eyes, try to feel the shift.

There's nothing. A feeling of wrongness rises in my chest, makes my throat go dry.

So no, I've never liked *The Tale of Dragons True*. It says things about who we are, what Sorrowfeld is, and sometimes those things don't quite match up with the way it feels to be barefoot on the cold castle floors, wearing a crown fit for someone else's head.

I hate that it's deciding I have to be someone new.

I hate that if I said, out loud, *I don't feel any different, I can't defeat a dragon*, Duke Verden would tell me the book knows better than I do.

"You're going to be such a boring princess," Lady Genevive says, but she's smiling, and I hope she's right. I hope I can be a boring princess who doesn't have to take on any dragons or save any kingdoms.

I hope the book is wrong.

Lady Genevive is the only friend I've ever had, and I'm not even really allowed to have her. Princesses aren't meant to have friends, but I suppose they make an exception for me, because of what happened to my family.

I look at them now—the portrait that hangs above the fireplace, the reason I love the castle library so much. Me, Mom, Dad, and my two older sisters, Princess Penelope and Princess Cassandra, who look like me but prettier, better, smarter. At the time of the portraits, I was two and Penelope and Cassandra were seven and ten. Which is awful, because that's younger than I am now. We are all in heavy silk gowns, and my sisters have on delicate tiaras and tiny earrings and a single necklace each—gold with a stone at the bottom. Red for Cassandra. A cloudy white for Penelope. And purple for me. Our birthstones.

If I spend enough time sitting across from their portraits, I almost remember them. People would say it's impossible—I was too young when the dragons took them, barely three years old—but I recall Penelope's singing voice, sweet and off tune, and Cassandra's way of knocking over vases because she could never seem to stop her body from jumping. I remember Mom's long fingers and Dad's silly bedtime stories, always about pirates and fairies and, yes, once in a while, even dragons.

I remember that he said he wasn't scared of them. He told a story about one named Bert, who lost his fire breath, and another named Leroy, who had a special blankie he slept with.

I remember that the first thing I asked when Sir Verden and Duchess Dutton told me my family was gone was *Did Bert do it? Or Leroy?*

Of course the dragons that did it fled, and I don't know their names or their favorite toys or anything about them at all, really, except that we were wrong to have been so brave about them. To have laughed away our fear. I was too young to know then what I know now.

There was no Bert. No Leroy. There were just dragons, cruel ones who wished to destroy us. People still talk about the day the dragons came—and the slow, awful realization that they must have flown away with my family.

We use words like *gone* and *taken*, but I'm pretty sure we mean *killed* and *dead*. We don't know exactly what happens to the people dragons capture, but we know they never return. We have annual holidays for those who have been taken by dragons over the decades—a knight who was about to get married, a townsperson who loved dancing, twin girls known as troublemakers. They have chapters in history books—we know more about the victims than we do about dragons. Aside from my birthday, dragons are rarely around. During big storms, they fly through the sky, liking the sound of thunder maybe. And every once in a while there is a broken roof, a toppled tree or tower, and the char of leaves or bark or grass left behind to tell us who did it.

And then there's my birthday, of course.

And the day they took my family.

Every time I think of it, I burn dragon-fire hot, my head feels too big to hold on to, my feet lose their grounding, I want to do nothing but hide in the darkest corner of the castle. I want it to be possible to hide from the things that might be true.

"We should do whatever you think would be the most fun for everyone else at the party," I say to Lady Genevive, who is still going on about cakes. "I won't be able to think about anything but dragons."

"It has to be magnificent," she says. "The biggest celebration in the history of Sorrowfeld." She is practically shaking with thrill. It makes me nauseous.

Lady Genevive has a crown of flowers in her thick black hair, but it's slightly askew, and her hair is wavy and knotted, and her silk dress is torn at the bottom. She lives with her family, Duke Verden and Duchess Dutton, in the north end of the castle, so that I don't have to live here alone. There are handmaidens and chefs and a great number of other people who do work in and around the castle, but with the exception of Lady Genevive and Duke Verden, they're all nervous around me, and they have been for all of the nine years since it happened, as if being the last remaining royal of Sorrowfeld means something very different than what it meant to be the youngest princess of Sorrowfeld.

That's fair, I guess.

I'll never really know what it would have been like, to forever simply be the youngest princess of Sorrowfeld. I only know this, here, now. That I am Princess Auden of Sorrowfeld, that I have ears that stick out and a heart-shaped birthmark on my shoulder and honey-colored hair and bangs that brush past my eyebrows and that for some reason, I am the princess the dragons didn't take.

Maybe they should have.

I know how to correctly curtsy to the royals of each of the neighboring kingdoms and what length and color of dress is right for every sort of occasion. But besides that, I'm not really sure who I am, and I don't think the kingdom is very sure either.

They're just waiting to find out.

Duke Verden has taught me how to read *The Tale of Dragons True* and how to memorize the history and rules written within. *Don't look dragons in the eyes*, he writes on a chalkboard in the library where we do our studies. *Don't give them names.*

Duchess Dutton has taught me to be refined and

elegant, to hold teacups gently and waltz with a straight back and nimble toes.

But Sorrowfeld has taught me that what they need me to be, in the face of losing the rest of the royal family, is perfect.

And even that might not be enough.

Chapter 8

Princess Auden
Two Hours Before the Swap

Duchess Dutton dresses me in ivory satin and yellow silk, colors she says are befitting a princess coming into herself.

"Aren't I already myself?" I ask. The ivory satin is soft on my skin, but the silk sash is tied too tightly. The shape of the gown is different than the little girl ones I've worn my whole life, and Duchess Dutton keeps adjusting it tighter and looser, up and down, like if she finds the exact right way for the fabric to drape and pull, I'll suddenly be all grown-up.

"You've been a child. You're becoming a young adult. Twelve, Princess Auden. Twelve is something new."

Duchess Dutton talks carefully. Everyone does, or at least thinks they do. But I can hear the things she wants in her voice now: *Is it true what the book says? Is twelve the age? Is she old enough at last to be useful?*

"It feels the same," I say. I don't want her to get excited. These last few months, the conversation has turned more and more to the idea of twelve, and the feeling around me has been desperate, eager, and hopeful. The hope is the worst part, because no matter how many new entries about the meaning of twelve appear in the book, I still feel exactly the same as always.

"Well, you're not twelve quite yet. A few more hours, right? Magic is quite precise, generally speaking," Duchess Dutton says. She holds me by the shoulders to look at the whole of me. She sees every wrinkle, every shoulder slump, every way I am not as good as my mother or sisters. She does not see the grip of my heart, the sweat on my neck, the sharp worry that when the dragons come today, they won't just take a look at me and fly off. They might stay.

Lady Genevive enters the room in her own gown. She's not a princess, so she is allowed to wear something less regal—green and purple and easy to walk in. "Everything's all set up. It's really pretty, Auden."

"Princess Auden," her mother corrects as she always does.

"Princess Auden," Lady Genevive says with a little roll of her eyes. I liked the way she said my name without my title. I'd like to know who that person is. Just Auden.

But I'll never find out.

On my last birthday, I'm not even sure that the dragons visiting was the worst thing to happen. They flapped their wings and spewed smoke like always, but at least they flew away. The conversation I heard Duke Verden having with a few of the Sorrowfeld subjects has stayed with me.

"She's lovely," a woman in a long gray dress said, frowning as if I wasn't lovely at all. "She's very refined. And loud. She knows how to speak up. A rare combination." Again, a frown. I hated how she said nice things in a mean way. "But we all know she wasn't really built for this. She's nothing like her mother. Nothing."

"She's learning," said Duke Verden. "She is. When the time comes, she'll be ready." He sounded as he always did—sure, solid. I tried to let myself think he could be right.

"I don't know," a man said, in a voice I can still hear right now in my head. "I want to believe the dragons left her here for a reason, but. Well. I just don't know that there's much there, underneath all the crowns and manners."

"Dragons always have a reason," Duke Verden said.

Then something else, in a lower whisper that I couldn't hear. I hoped it was something kind. But I worried and worried that it was the other thing—a truth about me that he knew, a way I was undeniably not enough.

Something around my jaw and behind my eyes tightened while listening to that conversation, and the dull, awful ache of it hasn't gone away since.

I can point my toes and brush my hair and sing the Sorrowfeld anthem in the most beautiful voice in the world, but it doesn't matter if I can't lead a kingdom. I'm good at the outside parts of being a princess, but deep down, like they said, there's not much there.

I straighten my skirt and touch my hair, my crown.

If I could choose, I'd be a regular girl in a regular family in a regular home with regular chores and thoughts and worries and hopes.

But I can't choose.

I am the remaining princess of Sorrowfeld.

I have to be something special.

Somehow.

Lady Genevive and Duchess Dutton lead me out of my tower, winding through the castle. The halls are chilly, the sunlight pokes in through stained-glass windows, everything is as it always is, me included. *Twelve, twelve, twelve,* my head says with every step, like if I focus on it enough it will somehow start to matter, the words in the book will come true, I will be the princess they need me to be, the princess Sorrowfeld deserves.

The doors to the grand ballroom open, revealing a room filled with candlelight, flowers, long tables set with silk tablecloths, golden utensils, and of course the crystal ceiling our castle is famous for. The room is always special, but today it's spectacular. Decorated for the most important birthday Sorrowfeld will ever see. The whole of Sorrowfeld leans forward to find out if today, finally, I am who they want me to be.

Chapter 9

Princess Auden
Thirty Minutes Before the Swap

I enter to the sound of trumpets, applause, and then the unsettled type of quiet that comes when everyone is waiting for magic to occur. I straighten my back and lift my chin.

I swallow. I don't much like parties, but no one has ever asked.

What I like to do most in the world is sit in my tower bedroom and watch a group of girls who live on the other side of the moat. They play games where they use sticks for swords, they paint their faces with berry juice, they stick their feet in the water, they laugh so hard they fall in. They make mud castles and dare each other to climb trees and do handstands. They play hide-and-seek. They are so regular and unbothered that it hurts to watch.

And yet I watch for hours, when I can.

I can't make mud castles or snort when I laugh. But I prefer bread and butter to toast and caviar. I take off my shoes in the castle yard and talk to butterflies and when I have trouble sleeping at night, most nights, I sing myself songs my parents sang me long, long ago.

My greatest wish is to not be a princess at all.

"The room looks lovely," I say instead of anything else.

The whole room is all hope and nerves—waiting for me to be spectacular, worried that I won't be.

I want to play in the moat. I want anything but this.

They all come every year, in spite of the dragons. Duke Verden has told them that this is how to honor the royalty that has vanished, by celebrating the one who remains. So they come. Watch the sky. Watch me.

But this year it's different. They are holding hands, smiling tensely, looking out the windows, at me, at the windows again. I've been waiting my whole life to be who they want me to be. And they've been promised today is the day. So have I.

It's impossible that a whole room of people are holding their breaths, but it feels that way. *Breathe*, I want to say. *Breathe, so that I can breathe.* Instead I wave and smile and straighten up even more than all the way up and stand next to Duke Verden for his annual speech.

"A kingdom without a princess is a kingdom at risk," Duke Verden says. His voice is deep, loud; it doesn't take much for him to command attention. I would have liked Duchess Dutton to give the first speech, or even Lady Genevive, although that sort of thing would be frowned upon. Even without a king, people look to the men in the room with the grayest hair, the deepest voices, the broadest shoulders. They're in charge.

Maybe it will change when I turn true. Maybe. The pages about twelve being a special age are so new, I don't know exactly what to expect. I will be the only one who can defeat a dragon. And I suppose that has to matter.

I don't want to battle dragons, but I don't want to fear them anymore either. And I certainly don't want to keep sitting on stacks of silk pillows, getting my nails painted, having my hair brushed, memorizing the names of princesses in other kingdoms. I want to do something.

I want to be someone worthy of being spared.

The dress feels too tight around my waist. My crown feels crooked. Duke Verden doesn't notice. He continues on.

"When the three princesses of Sorrowfeld were born, one after the other over the years, we felt so blessed. We would have an abundance of princesses. A kingdom of princesses. We never imagined we would be left waiting for our Princess Auden to come of age. But in our grief, we raised her. And now it is her twelfth birthday. And our enchanted text tells us this is the moment we've been waiting for."

The crowd nods. Looks at me. Squints.

Still, I am certain they don't breathe, not a single one of them.

Terror fizzes inside me. I feel exactly as I've always felt. Exactly like myself. It's awful.

Duke Verden turns to Duchess Dutton instead of me. He gestures for her to address the room. I barely need to be here, except I am also, somehow, the star of the show.

"This is the moment," Duchess Dutton says. She pauses. "The dragons are on their way. You are twelve. Tonight you'll defeat them."

My dress feels heavy and sweaty. It's too clingy and too poufy and all wrong. I want my hair reconfigured— down instead of up, or straight instead of curled. I want to be entirely different and far, far away from this, from everything that's led me exactly here.

I know what's expected, but we are nearing the moment I turn twelve and there's nothing, nothing. Just me.

I've said yes to everything my whole life, and everyone's loved that about me, but maybe, maybe, I can try saying something different today. Maybe that's what my parents would have wanted me to do. I take a breath and steady myself. I have so little time left to change the course of the day.

"I don't know that the book meant the second I turned twelve I'd have to—" I try to put on my princess poise, but it's hard, they're all hand-wringing and window-watching and I am thumping, all of me, head, heart, limbs, mind. "I don't think it said that on a princess's twelfth birthday she saves her kingdom. It doesn't say that."

I try to remember the exact words that appeared less than a year ago like an awful threat. *Only a true princess can defeat a dragon. A true princess is not a child anymore. A princess turns true at twelve.*

It does not say a true princess **has to** defeat a dragon right away, it doesn't say anywhere that a princess's birthday is for doing the impossible. But Duke Verden is already shaking his head like I'm too silly, too young to know what he knows.

"Why would we wait for them to attack us unprepared? Or wait for another birthday? Why would we wait, when you are ready now?" He sounds scared, Duke Verden. Maybe even a little desperate. He's been on edge lately, hunching over *The Tale of Dragons True*, searching the sky for dragons, asking me over and over and over if I'm ready.

I never answer.

Until now.

"I understand the text. And you're all here, which is—it's very lovely, and I thank you for, um, that. But the truth is I don't feel any different," I say. "Maybe it takes a few days to settle in. I'm not ready quite yet. I'm sorry. I understand what is meant to happen. But it hasn't. Yet."

"Princess Auden," Duchess Dutton says, her hand grabbing my elbow. Her eyebrows are alarmed, her grip is urgent. "Don't do this," she whispers.

But it's too late, they all hear us, there is nothing else for them to watch. This is the only thing to care about. A dragon is going to fly overhead any moment. What's the use in lying to a whole kingdom about whether I think I can defeat it?

Duke Verden starts to speak, his face turning an angry red. I interrupt him, which I have never done before, but I find it feels good right now. "You yourself have told me that not every word of *The Tale of Dragons True* is exactly literally the truth," I say. "That we have to be careful in how we interpret it." I'm saying more than I am supposed to, but he taught me to speak clearly, hold my ground. He must not have thought I'd ever do it against him.

Everyone in this room knows there are parts of the book we don't trust, parts that don't line up correctly with what we've always known. The chapters on dragons that used to be humans, of course. Strange maps of worlds we've never seen. A treatise, once, on why princesses should lose their standing, and fairies or unicorns or sea witches should take over. We have always been careful to interpret the enchanted text with care, to parse every word and line it up with what we know.

And Duke Verden has always been the person we turn to, to help us know what to believe.

"Why is this any different?" I ask.

"You yourself know that you are no expert on ancient enchanted texts, Princess Auden. I have studied my whole life—dedicated myself to you and this kingdom. I cannot believe you would question me. Have I not earned your respect?"

The people of Sorrowfeld nod, agreeing with him.

Duchess Dutton's lips are pursed, her arms crossed, unhappy with the lack of propriety the duke and I are showing.

Princesses don't apologize, so I do not say I'm sorry. I'm not sorry. I am furious. Duke Verden is the expert on *The Tale of Dragons True*, but am I not the expert on my own self? I organize the vibrating thoughts into something calm, royal, but before I can get the words out, Duke Verden stops me. "They're coming," he says. "It's not the time to debate."

"I—" My throat feels as though it's closing. I shut my eyes tight like I might open them to become the right thing, a grown princess. But nothing in me feels lit up or shining or new. I don't suddenly know how to defeat a dragon. I'm the same disappointing leftover princess I've always been.

"Surely you feel it," Duchess Dutton says as she adjusts my crown, pushing it more securely onto my head. I am perfectly dressed. I look exactly right. Princesses wear silver slippers. They curtsy. They play the flute. They fight dragons.

But I still feel like a kid—with bruises on my knees and a knot in my hair and a hankering for chocolate cookies and bedtime stories.

"I don't know," I say, hoping they'll accept that as an answer this time.

"It will happen," she says, and it sounds like a promise I never made that I'm somehow in charge of keeping. "The book says twelve. And here you are. Twelve."

I never want to hear the word *twelve* again.

The room has been filled with things I love: tall candles and tablecloths made of silver silk, and flowering vines and tiny vanilla cakes and birds in cages—thrushes, for their beautiful tunes, which they are singing out now.

Impossibly, the people of Sorrowfeld rush to eat, to go through the steps of the party, like maybe that will shove me into trueness. The dragons flap closer and closer, but we sit in the castle and pretend this is a party for a few more minutes, while we can, I suppose.

There are berries and chocolates and cheeses and the most delicious, warm bread that almost makes the whole thing worth it. I sit by myself at the table that was built to fit a whole family, in a golden throne originally fashioned for Mom. All the seats at my table are left empty, usually, aside from mine. A reminder of who's missing.

I've been eating at tables alone for my whole life, but today feels different. Maybe I'm really becoming a princess, because when the sad feeling of sitting by myself and watching the rest of the banquet hall chatter sinks in and the sound of dragons grows louder, maybe I *do* change a little, just not in the way they hope.

I'm sitting in a room of people who want me to fight a dragon and save their homes, their lives. But I'm not allowed to do what I want? I'm not allowed to sit with a friend?

I stand up.

I will show them what it is to be a princess, at least for one tiny moment. My heart is sprinting, my hands are gulfs of sweat. I need someone near me.

"Lady Genevive, please join me at the royal table," I say in a voice that perhaps is the voice of a princess. It feels low in my chest, and my toes all squeeze together from the newness of it.

At the other tables, the full ones where people are allowed to eat together, be together, celebrate me together, eyebrows spike. Shoulders tense. Chins jut forward, others sink back; every person startles in some large or tiny way.

"Can I?" Lady Genevive asks her mother. But before Duchess Dutton has a chance to answer, I answer instead.

"Of course you can. You must. It's an order. From a princess."

And so she does.

Chapter 10

Princess Auden
The Swap

Castle workers bring Lady Genevive heavy forks and heavier plates, and she says thank you, but she's shaking, fidgeting in the enormous royal chairs, scratching her chin, her forehead, her thighs, as if she's allergic to this whole situation.

I relate.

"I shouldn't be here, it's not appropriate," she says.

"It's my birthday. I'm tired of eating alone. If I'm going to be a true princess, shouldn't I get to decide things?"

"I suppose," Lady Genevive says. She shrugs and her voice is mouse-tiny and I wonder if my sisters would have been full-voiced, straight-backed, sure of themselves. I try to be those things. I cut my meat carefully, chew without opening my mouth, dab my chin with the silk napkin.

I'm not sure any of it matters, though.

"What's this?" Lady Genevive says. She points at something by my plate that I hadn't noticed. A small present wrapped in gold paper, tied with a white ribbon but no card. It could be from anyone, and it's not traditional to give a princess gifts on her birthday. A princess's birthday is about her subjects, not herself.

And in the case of my birthday, of course, it's about dragons.

Still, it's nice to have a gift. I think if Mom and Dad were here, maybe they would have insisted upon a small present for each of their daughters on their birthdays. The rule about a birthday being about the kingdom seems like the sort of thing Duke Verden cares about more than anyone else.

"Is it from you?" I ask Lady Genevive hopefully. But she shakes her head.

Maybe I shouldn't open it without checking with the duke, the duchess, someone else. But how can I turn true if I'm still acting like a kid, waiting for everyone else to give me instructions? A princess, a real one, would do what she wants. A princess would know what is rightly hers.

"Well, let's see what it is," I say in the voice a princess

might have. I unwrap it carefully, and I'm not sure what I'm hoping it will be, but I hadn't imagined what it actually is.

It is small and round. Not made from brass or rubies. Not delicately carved or adorned with anything sparkling or lush. It is shiny and flimsy. It is a shade of pink—a bright, upsetting color—I have never seen before. It feels breakable, but not the way a crystal goblet does. There on its surface is a bright yellow, crudely drawn face—just two dots and a curved line for a smile.

The object is ugly, yes, but also upsetting in its ugliness. Unusual and wrong. I turn it over and discover a reflective surface on the other side. A small mirror, made to fit in a pocket, which is a lovely idea, but why would it be made with such strange craftsmanship, such disturbing design?

"What *is* that?" Lady Genevive asks. I love her for the way she can wear things like disgust right on her face. I try to cover up my confusion.

In case of something.

Before I can think of what that something is, there is a burst of fire lighting up the windows.

The room gasps, even though we've all been waiting for exactly this moment. Lady Genevive screams, and I consider, for a moment, running. And hiding. But where?

There's nowhere to go. There's nowhere to hide.

So quickly, Duke Verden is at my side, a heavy hand on my shoulder, pushing me a little toward the dragons.

"You are going to save us," he says. "You are going to defeat them." He tries to say it like he's sure, but still there is that wave of fear in the certainty. "Remember the rules. Don't look at them directly. Their fires will burn hotter. They will get angrier. Do not ever look at a dragon directly. Do not say their names. Or any names at all."

I nod. I know the rules. I've heard them for years.

Inside me, nothing has changed. I am Auden. I have beautiful manners and know how to waltz. I love rules and the way it feels to see Duke Verden nod slowly when I follow them correctly.

There's another flash of fire. Chairs scrape on the floor, people run to the center of the room to be together, to wait for me to fix it.

My heart presses against itself. A stripe of sweat forms on my back and I straighten, as if it is commanding me to do so. I am not supposed to be angry. Princesses don't rage. They don't worry. They don't doubt or hesitate or wish that they could just eat birthday cake and forget about the rest.

Princesses fight. They save. They conquer and defend. This is what I've been told, so it must be what is true.

Even so.

"They're here every year," I say, and my voice sounds screechier, wilder than it ever has. "The book didn't used to say twelve. Maybe it will change again."

"Princess Auden. It is not like you to be argumentative about your duties. We are depending on you." His voice cracks in a way I've never heard. It has always been Duke Verden who is most afraid of the dragons. Duke Verden who opens *The Tale of Dragons True* daily to see if there is more information on how we will handle them. Duke Verden here, now, taking me by the shoulders and facing my body toward the windows, which are darkening by the moment.

Smoke starts to fill the banquet hall, a smell I both remember and don't, like something from a dream I'm not sure I ever dreamed. Outside I can see their giant wings, their glittering scales.

I look to the grown-ups—Duke Verden and Duchess Dutton and the rest of them, the people of Sorrowfeld who claim to have raised me, the ones who visit the graves of my family and promise to watch out for me, but who now all stand in the middle of the room, looking at me expectantly. Like I'm an appointment they made months ago. Something they are sure they are owed.

Most years, the dragons come, frighten us all, circle the castle for a few minutes, come to the windows, make loud sounds, and pour fire into the air. They have destroyed other kingdoms. And over the centuries, they have knocked down many parts of ours. One wing of the castle, since rebuilt. A forest of trees, now covered in new growth.

But on my birthday, there is never anything but fire in the air, terror, and the promise that they'll come back.

We don't know why they come on my birthday, or what they are looking for, or why they ultimately leave us alone. But we know someday they will do what they've always intended to do—try to destroy us all. Like they've done to other kingdoms. Like Duke Verden has warned us about.

"Let's finish this today, Princess Auden," Duke Verden says. "Once and for all." He's so terrified, even his beard is twitching, his hands rubbing each other, his thighs, the back of his neck, the top of his head. "You're twelve. You're ready."

I hate the way he keeps saying "twelve," like it means childhood is over. I think of those girls across the moat. I could scream.

But there are all these faces looking at me like I could change everything, like they need me. And I can't ever be a girl playing in the moat, as badly as I want to be. I can't be a princess with a family. I can't be anything I want to be, but I could be what *they* want me to be, maybe.

Maybe.

My chest is tight, my head is pounding. There are so few options. Or maybe there aren't any.

So I do the one thing I know to do. I run outside. Lady Genevive calls after me; so does Duchess Dutton, panicking but not actually stopping me.

This is my destiny, isn't it? Maybe I will feel like a princess when I reach the lawn, when I see the dragons' faces.

Maybe the dragons will make it clear what I am meant to do, what sort of dance we are destined to wind up in.

The air outside is cool. Misty. It smells like fire. Dragons haunt the skies, their wings flapping out enormous gusts of wind. A smarter princess than me would have grabbed a sword, a club, a match, anything at all to try to fight them. But all I have is the strange shiny mirror that got caught in the palm of my hand while we watched the dragons take over the skies. I catch a glimpse of myself in it for only an instant. I am sweating in ruffles and silk. I am wild-eyed and scared. I am surrounded by a sky full of dragons.

And then I am gone.

The Tale of Dragons True

Denny, age 7

This book is only about Sorrowfeld.

Nothing else belongs here.

Keep out, rest of the world.

Chapter 11

Denny Greene

A lilac-stoned castle. Tall turrets. A grassy hill. A glittering moat.

A dragon with flapping wings above me.

A dragon!

But no. It cannot be a dragon because it cannot be a castle because I cannot be in a long silk dress and a heavy golden crown.

Shouts come from the castle windows, heads peeking out with worried expressions on their faces. There are other faces, too, with expressions more in line with the way people look when they're watching the last few minutes of the town football games.

The dragon snorts fire, flaps her wings harder, rears her head back. Behind her are three more in various shades and sizes. The one closest to me lands on the tallest turret for a moment, her body so large I'm surprised she doesn't crush the building—the building! My building! I recognize its shade of lilac, its many towers. It's mine!—but she seems to be resting on it lightly, a choice she's making to wait before destroying it. She tilts her head like she needs to see me from other angles in order to know what to do with me.

For a moment, everything else stops. My body can't move, my chin points up, up at the sky. My arms hang at my sides.

Mom used to give me one of her special just-you-and-me smiles when I said the word *awesome*.

Really, Den? she'd ask. *That hamburger fills you with a sense of awe?* It was half joke and half lesson. That's how Mom used to be. Funny and smart and annoying and right about a lot.

But this—this is awe. I am in awe.

A dragon.

My head stops swimming for long enough to take her in, to find her magnificent. Because she is. She's an orangey, shiny shade of pink, and her wings are the largest part of her, but more delicate than I would have thought. She's everything and nothing like I imagined.

She's perfect.

And in one single swipe, she could kill me.

A dragon! A dragon! My heart beats, thrill and fear and pride all at once.

"Come *back*!" a voice calls, a young one this time, young but more forceful than the others, more certain that my returning is the right thing to do. It's enough to shake off the awe and wonder and bring me back to the terror.

I'm not at home. I'm not in Magnolia Bend. I can feel the heat of the dragon's breath. The earth is trembling from its power.

On shaky legs, I follow the pleading, pretty voice to the door of the castle, and the dragon stays, watching the way my body moves, the rhythm I run in, the shape my arms make. It feels awful to be watched like that by a creature breathing fire, curling its claws, making a tornado from the flap of its wings.

But also, it's how I would like to watch the dragon. From a distance. And with that level of focus, that sort of time to take it all in.

A dragon, my breath says again. And my eyes fill with tears at the beauty and horror and impossibility of it.

The door to the castle—*my castle! Sorrowfeld's castle!*—is heavy, but I get it open and throw my body inside. Once there, my gaze lands on a girl. She's messy haired and crying. Her face is Runa-shaped, her hair Runa-colored. She throws her arms around my neck and clings. "Princess Auden! I was so scared! What happened? They're leaving? Does that mean they're defeated? I thought it would be different from other years, maybe a battle or something. Are we okay?"

I have a hundred replies and a thousand questions, but I need to see if she's right, if the dragon has actually flown away, so I stand on my tiptoes to look out the too-high castle window. There's smoke and dust dragged up by the flapping of wings, and there's a tree that's fallen, and there's the four dragons, but now they are off in the distance, flying away.

"They're gone," I say, relieved and sad at once. I want Runa here. I want to show her the castle, the dragons, the world we made. She's the only one who could understand.

"You did it!" the girl cheers. "She did it!" She must expect a swell of applause because she pauses like something special is coming, but nothing does.

"That was not a defeat," a somber voice says. It belongs to a gray-haired, gray-bearded man whose face is stony and sad. "They leave every year. They still roam this earth. They will return."

The girl shifts closer to me and grabs my hand. Hers is the same size as mine and warm. I know without knowing that she is a friend. I don't understand how I'm here, in this place, but just as I recognize the shape of the castle, the look of the dragons, I know that this girl—breathing hard from panic, dark hair and unexpected freckles covering her whole face, hand squeeze-squeeze-squeezing mine like it's telling me a message—is a good, true friend.

"Lady Genevive," a woman covered in the same freckles with the same sweet voice says, "let's leave Princess Auden to talk to Father for a bit. They have serious things to discuss."

"Denny," I mumble.

"What's that?" She must be my new friend—Genevive's—mother.

"I go by Denny."

She squints. Genevive laughs. The man with the booming voice and serious face clears his throat.

"You're not feeling well," Genevive's mother says. "Of course you're not. It's been a difficult day for us all."

"Denny's a cute name," Genevive says, but her mother gives her a look, and she bows her head. "Not for a princess, of course. But cute. Maybe we should name one of the royal horses that."

I think I should be insulted that the name I've been called my entire life is only befitting of a smelly animal, but Genevive doesn't say it the way Sadie might, like it's meant to be pointy and prickly and mean. She says it like an offering, a gift of some kind.

"Sure," I say. "A horse. Cool."

There's a pause again. The same squint from Genevive's mom, like something is off. And of course something *is* off. Me. I am the off thing. I'm in a castle surrounded by people in petticoats and jewels. I stood face-to-face with a dragon. The earth is scorched. The skies are smoky. My garden shed is gone.

And there is a crown on my head.

I close my eyes like it all might go away, but when I open them again, I am still in this new world.

New, but familiar. The castle I've drawn a hundred times. The dragons were larger-than-life renditions of ones I've sculpted out of clay. My heart absolutely will not stop pounding.

"*Cool.*" Genevive repeats what I've said, like she's never heard the word before but likes it. Smiling the kind of smile Runa might give me after telling me a secret. Then Genevive leaves with her mother, and I'm alone with the serious man and his serious beard and the serious way he says what I guess is my name.

"Princess Auden. I do not know what happened out there, or why they spared us once again. But you cannot be impulsive like that. You are bringing danger on us all. I have seen princesses defeat dragons in my day, in other kingdoms far from here. I don't know how they do it. But I do know it is not like *that*, running out of rooms without a word. They think. They are deliberate. They do what they have been brought up to do. Do you understand?"

I do *not* understand. I don't know who this man is or what he's saying. I don't even know who I am anymore.

"I'm sorry," I whisper. "I don't know what's going on."

"Princess Auden. We have let you be a child all these years, waiting for you to grow up. And now here you are, twelve. And here the dragons are. Your mother and father and sisters, whether they be dead or alive, are counting on you to avenge them. We are counting on you to save Sorrowfeld. You are not a child anymore. Do you hear me?"

Everyone in the castle can hear him, I assume. His voice booms off the walls, echoes in my ears. His words don't make sense, though. I'm twelve here, just like I am in real life. Twelve *is* a child. Not old enough to avenge anyone. Not old enough to save a kingdom or even myself.

My heart lurches, a nauseous feeling that's in my chest instead of my stomach. Back home, sometimes, Dad looks at me the way this man is looking at me—like I can do something big to help, like I can save us all. I try to scrunch the feeling up and forget it, but somehow, so far from home I'm not even sure how I got here, I am still expected to be someone better than I am.

"Sorrowfeld is counting on you," the man says.

Another gigantic heart lurch.

Last week, Dad asked me if Mom and I had had a fight, and if I could go make up with her if we had. He said that would make her feel better. He said spending time with me was one of the only things that helped her.

Maybe he meant it to be nice, but it felt just like this.

My hands make fists of themselves. I look at the color of the castle stones, the shape of the turrets I can see from the window, the shade of my dress, the size of the golden throne in the corner.

My legs wobble. The gray-haired serious-faced man looks at me harder and harder, like the strength of his gaze might upend me, might turn me into the princess he keeps saying I am.

It doesn't, though. I am solidly Denny, just in silk and emeralds.

I cannot save a kingdom. I cannot defeat a dragon. I can't even save my mother or make her stop drinking, not this time, and I can't fix my friendship with Runa or keep a twelfth birthday party from being an absolute disaster. The dress I'm in is itchy, and the crown hurts my head.

They gray-haired serious-mouthed man leans down so his face is closer to mine, so that his words are a secret between us. "You failed today. You were not the princess we needed. Do not let it happen again."

The Tale of Dragons True

Denny, age 9

Witch Rules

1. The witch can't leave her castle.
2. The witch can enchant the Lake of Leer to do her bidding.
3. The witch must answer any questions royalty ask.
4. Any curse a witch places must have a way to be broken.

Chapter 12

Princess Auden

Brown.

It's all brown and unattractive and uncomfortable and small. I know, of course I do, that not everyone lives in castles. The girls I watch across the moat, and all the other people of Sorrowfeld, have homes, regular ones, I suppose, though I've never visited inside them. From the outside, they are gray and vine-covered and sweet-looking. I don't think they look like this, with wide-slatted floors and dusty patches and things stuck to the walls and rags as curtains and not even a bed upon which to sleep.

I sit up.

Perhaps the dragons brought me here. Or the witch. Maybe this is where dragons keep princesses who have failed to defeat them. A cursed shack in the middle of nowhere. I have never been told stories of failed princesses, but I know they must exist because of the worried way Duchess Dutton talks about my destiny with dragons.

Maybe—it hurts to even think of this possibility, hope having always been an aching spot around my heart and in my lungs—my family is here. Maybe the dragons kept them alive, maybe I am moments away from seeing them, even. My whole self hums with the impossible dream of it.

They're probably dead, I remind myself. *Vanished means gone forever.*

Still. The hope keeps on humming.

"Denny? Can I come in?" The voice is male, a tenor maybe, not the bellowing baritone of Duke Verden, not the gravelly voice I remember my father having, but something different and brand-new.

I straighten my body and ready myself for battle. Maybe this is it? This is the mystery of turning true? You are transported elsewhere to battle?

The door opens and I brace for a dragon, but it is a man. A man in strange rags, with hair that needs combing and a look on his face I've never seen before—something shy and shamed and sad.

"Mom's fine," he says.

The words are like a wave hitting shore, except I am

the shore. I am all sand and seashells and the shock of the cold water. I don't have a mom. Such a sentence has not been said to me since I was too little to even know about dragons and death and duty.

"And what is it you know of my mother, kind sir?" I try. I have always been good at the manners of princessdom, and Duke Verden has assured me they are necessary skills.

The man startles. "Kind sir? I like that."

"If you know where my mother is, please reveal her to me. I believed her to be gone forever." My voice breaks a little on the word *forever*. It always does.

"Denny. Don't say that. Even if it feels that way today, you know that's not true."

"Who's Denny?"

"Oh," the man says, something like a smirk, but kinder, moving his mouth. "Are you going by Auden now? That's what Runa told me."

"Princess Auden," I correct him. He must be a villager, perhaps one who has been gone a long time, who doesn't remember all the rules of royalty. He hasn't bowed.

"Well. Princess. Who knew. Come inside, sweetheart, okay? We should have some cake. Mom's up for it."

"We are inside."

This man in rags speaks in riddles, and I wonder

if this is a test of some kind, a part of my journey to defeating the dragons. It has the feeling of a witch's curse, the sort of tricky game she will throw you into, filled with puzzles and complications and quests. Like the Witch's Wander.

I steady myself. Look around. There are dragon drawings everywhere. A painting of the Lake of Leer on the wall. Yes. This must be the witch's doing.

"Well, come inside the house," the man says, shaking his head like I am the one riddling. He walks away from the tiny home, and I peek out, seeing if I am meant to follow him. A few steps away, there is another house. It is something beige and square and red-doored. It is odd, but the rest of the street is covered with houses that look remarkably similar—different shades of beige, different doors, different sizes of windows, but all sort of half echoes of one another.

I follow him to the home and enter through the red door. Inside, patterns and colors abound. Things are shiny and noisy. There's a wooden table with wooden chairs around it and a woman in a nightgown in one of the chairs.

She could be a ghost, perhaps, but I know without being told that this is the one he has been speaking of. The mom. There is a cake in the center of the table, and she looks at it like she isn't sure what its purpose is.

"I'm doing my best," she says in a voice that is feathery and sad. Defeated. "I'm doing my best, and you hated your party anyway."

I think of my party—fresh flowers and piles of food and iridescent table linens and the *thwap thwap* of dragon wings threatening us. I wonder if the party here was similar. It's hard to tell. There are some streamers. Bowls of neon-colored snacks. Furniture that looks pushed aside, out of place, the memory of people having filled the room.

"I don't think I hated it," I say. I don't know what is going on here exactly, but it seems the polite thing to say. And she's so sad and small, I want to be kind.

The man serves me a slice of cake. The woman droops. The man looks back and forth between us, like something is supposed to happen, something magical, something to make the moment better.

"We should sing!" the dad says, too excited for the size of the room, the way it feels. I can't imagine singing.

The mom shakes her head. Gets up from the table. "Just stop. You don't want me here anyway," she says, her voice quivery and sad, but it's a strange thing to say, because she never seemed very *here* at all. "I'm just ruining it." She puts her plate down and leaves the table, walking slowly up the stairs.

"Honey. We love you. Stay."

"I said STOP!" she yells, gripping the banister, her body wobbling for a moment like she might topple. Then she straightens herself and finishes the climb up the stairs.

The sound of that yelled *stop* feels like it's echoing. It was loud and awful.

The dad slumps. "She's going to be fine, Denny," he says to me in a voice that doesn't believe itself. "She got better before. She will do it again. She loves you so much."

In Sorrowfeld we don't ever say loving someone will stop them from being ill, but with the right enchantment, I suppose anything is possible.

"So love will— She just needs love?" I want to understand what curse this family is under, what the witch has thrown me into.

The dad looks confused, like he doesn't know the answer to the question, and my eyes search the room for a book that might explain the rules to me. There is always a way to break a curse. Witches are required to give a way out.

"Among other things," the dad says. But he doesn't say what the other things are. A sliver of a flower petal from the tallest mountain? An eyelash from a centaur? A cup of water from the Lake of Leer? I wait for him to hand me a scroll with a list, but he just looks down, then away, out the window.

Something near my heart gives, softens a little, and aches in a brand-new way. *I am supposed to be fighting a dragon*, I want to say. I almost say it. But the dad looks so drawn, so tired, that I stay quiet instead. Maybe I can do what he is asking. Give enough love to save this woman. It must be easier, mustn't it, than saving a kingdom? It might be nice, really, to have a break from being a princess. To let someone else fight the dragons.

I take another piece of cake.

It's delicious.

The Tale of Dragons True

Denny and Runa, age 8

The grass turns pink at night. Fairies paint it that way. They make houses from blades of grass. Then they fly the houses up into the treetops and hang them there. There is one tree that a thousand fairies have hung their houses on.

In Sorrowfeld, you eat cake every day.

In Sorrowfeld, you wash your hair in the moat and can decide what color it should be.

In Sorrowfeld, you ride a unicorn to the market.

In Sorrowfeld, everything is made of gold, pretty much.

In Sorrowfeld, princesses sleep in the tallest tower up the twistiest stairs.

In Sorrowfeld

Chapter 13

Denny Greene

"You need sleep," Genevive's mother says. The castle is clearing of people and of decorations. Villagers in simple brown and tan and gray outfits carry bundles out with them—flowers and linens and uneaten food and tiny cakes. There's a sadness to it. I know what it looks like when something has been hoped for but never happened.

It looks like this.

We didn't write much about disappointment in Sorrowfeld. We wrote parties that lasted all night, and balls where princesses met princes. We wrote birthdays that unicorns visited and long afternoons talking to fairies by the moat. We didn't write about dragons that couldn't be defeated or waiting for a special day that isn't right at all. I want to take out a pen and scribble over their sadnesses, make it all magical, the way it was when we first started writing about Sorrowfeld.

Before I got so fixated on dragons.

Before Runa decided twelve changed everything.

I want to visit the Sorrowfeld we wrote when we were very, very young.

In this Sorrowfeld, people look at the ground. Duchess Dutton is one big frown. Her dress is beautiful—pearls circling around the neck and sleeves and waist, green and gold silk bunching and draping in unusual ways, the skirt puffing out so wide people have to step aside to make room for her. But she's deflating in that beautiful dress.

"I'm sorry," I say, because she so obviously wanted a day that fit the dress, and instead she got dragons and my confusion and this awkward ending, where everyone in ball gowns slumps out of the castle, only a few of us remaining.

"I'm sorry, *Duchess Dutton*," she says, a correction that is delivered firmly. She sounds like someone who corrects people often.

"I'm sorry, Duchess Dutton," I repeat. Trying to be better comes naturally to me, too. She puts a hand on my back, asking it to straighten, so I straighten. She tucks a hair behind my ear, so I do the other side. It doesn't take much to make her happy, and she smiles.

"See? You're a real princess now," she says. "You just need to act like it."

"Yes, Duchess Dutton," I say, and she smiles again.

"Tomorrow we need to talk to the kingdom. You need to assure them that all will be right. That you have become a real princess at the exact age of twelve, just as Duke Verden predicted you would. The dragons have left for the time being. You are a true princess now. When they return, you'll defeat them."

Duchess Dutton's eyes are a solid gray. She doesn't leave any room for disagreements or questions of what she's saying.

"I'll defeat them?" I ask anyway. Her chin stiffens.

"It is your destiny, isn't it?"

I can't tell if the question is real or rhetorical, so I shrug.

"Princesses do not shrug," I'm reminded.

I'm not a princess, I want to say. *I'm Denny. I shrug. I shrug more than basically anything else. I'm Denny, and I don't belong here.*

I don't say those things, though. They're true, but it is also true that I don't belong at home. In Magnolia Bend, twelve-year-old girls like taking selfies and wearing bras. They are talking about the school dance, the very first one, that will happen in a few weeks. They want to have a first kiss. They wear clips in their hair and uncomfortable shoes, and they know the words to songs I don't really like.

"What do you think I should do now that I'm a true princess?" I ask. This is wrong too, I can tell by Duchess Dutton's sigh.

"True princesses wouldn't ask that," she says. I'm tired of answers like this. She sounds like Dad, wanting me to know something I can't possibly know if no one ever explains it to me.

I almost become my own slumped girl in a ball gown, but I'm not in Magnolia Bend trying to figure out my mom and how to fix her or Runa and how to keep her. I'm in Sorrowfeld.

Maybe here I *do* know what to do. After all, I've spent years thinking about princesses and how they're supposed to act, and Sorrowfeld and how it's supposed to be, and dragons and what to expect of them.

I want that to be enough, but all those things I wrote and imagined don't feel the same here, in the real place, with the real people, with the actual dragons darkening the sky.

"Please help Princess Auden remember herself," Duchess Dutton says to Genevive, who has come to stand with us. Duchess Dutton puts the same hand on the same part of Genevive's back. Just like me, she straightens, looking immediately more regal, more sophisticated. Duchess Dutton marches off, throwing out orders to people in plain clothes about what to do with certain plates, certain pastries, certain chairs and tables that are now being gruntingly moved aside, carried to other rooms, other parts of this enormous castle.

"You made her mad," Genevive says. Her eyebrows slope like Runa's. Her mouth smiles like Runa's—first closed lips, then a bigger smile that looks almost accidental, the way it leaps onto her face.

"Runa? Is it you?" I ask. "Is it us? And now we're here?"

"I'm sorry?" Genevive's smile shifts quickly into concern.

"Runa?" I say again, hoping to see something more like recognition on her face. I want her to lean in, like this whole thing is a big secret, and tell me what we're doing here, why our invented dragon-filled world has become real. Maybe this is my birthday gift. Maybe this is a dream. Maybe this is something she has been grappling with for months, not knowing how to tell me. Maybe this is why things have been so strange between us.

"I don't know what *runa* means," she says, and as she

says it, the things that look exactly like my best friend seem to shift. What seemed so familiar for a moment is gone, and now she is just a girl in Runa's approximate shape and style, but dressed in a gown and looking ruffled and unsure next to me.

Just like in Magnolia Bend, she and I are not in whatever this is together. Not anymore. I'm on my own.

"I . . . I guess I'm tired," I say. "From the party?"

"It was a big day," Genevive says. "The party. The dragons. You'll be able to get them, right? Now that you're twelve?"

"Do you really think twelve is . . . I mean, twelve is kind of young, right? To do . . . that?"

Genevive looks at me the same way Runa has been looking at me lately—like I'm missing something, like we aren't quite in the same moment, somehow.

"I don't think I know how to be a princess," I say. I'm in Sorrowfeld, a world I invented. Surely I can at least speak the truth here, even if I can't back home.

"I suppose you wish your sisters could help you," Genevive says. "I shall certainly try to help, of course. But I'm not—I'm not a princess."

"Right," I say, trying to keep track of the things I'm learning. Genevive is not a princess. She is not Runa. She is my friend. She might be able to help. I had sisters, but maybe I don't anymore. The dragons are coming for me, they have always been coming for me. But now I maybe have to kill them? I am a princess. A lot is expected of me.

"Shall we retire to your chambers?" she asks. It is going to take a lot to learn to speak like her.

"Sure," I say.

"Yes, Lady Genevive," she says, in the same firm teaching voice her mother used only minutes before. I swallow.

"Yes, Lady Genevive," I say. She puts a hand on my back. I straighten. This is what it is to be a princess, I guess.

She leads me to my room. She didn't have to, though. I know every step of the way. I have drawn this castle and its turrets and towers over and over again for years. I am, sort of, somehow, home.

Chapter 14

Denny Greene

I sleep on a bed of feathers and wake up sore-backed and sleepy-eyed. This is being a princess too, I guess. At first glance, everything is wonderful in my new princess room. The bed is so tall I have to climb a golden step stool to reach it. It looks soft and fluffy, covered in blankets made of fur and silk. They are thick and slippery and golden and late-summer-blueberry purple and after-storm-ocean blue.

But they're hot all piled on top of me, and the bed is so soft it feels like it can barely hold me up. I can't sleep. The world is too intense, too *real* for something I made up with Runa. Playwrights get to see their imagined worlds come to life onstage, but this is so much more than that. This isn't a set built by people who wear measuring tapes around their necks and hammers at their waists. These aren't actors trying out lines. This is real. The sheets. The sky. Lady Genevive.

The dragons.

Lady Genevive knocks on the door and slips into the room, but the moment she sees me, her face shifts into worry. For an actress, I must be doing an awful job of pretending to be okay.

"Have you taken ill, Princess Auden?" she asks. "Shall I call the royal examiner? You don't look well at all."

"I'm just tired," I say, yawning. Lady Genevive looks away from the wideness of my mouth. I guess princesses don't yawn, either.

"You need sleep. To defeat dragons, you must be well rested."

"Okay."

"And a big breakfast. The chef is preparing crepes and porridge and a warm chocolate soup. Would you like anything else?"

"Warm chocolate soup? Like . . . hot chocolate?"

"Are you officially renaming it?" Lady Genevive asks. Her eyes keep darting around the room like she's looking for something solid but isn't finding it. "Shall I alert the royal naming committee? They are always happy to have input from you."

I have no idea what to say to that, so she keeps going.

"Although I guess you should focus more on the dragons than on renaming soups. I'm sure you understand."

I nod. Dragons are more important than soup. Yes. I can agree with that.

I'd thought Genevive was my friend. Or, well, not my friend, but the princess's friend, which was good enough for me. But this morning she is less friend and more some sort of assistant I didn't ask for. She beckons for other people to come into my room, and three girls arrive—all around my age, wearing matching light gray skirts and white tops and silent smiles. They have beautiful fabrics draped across their arms—as lovely as the pile of blankets on my bed.

"What shall we be wearing today, Princess Auden?" one of the girls asks. "I thought perhaps periwinkle for the morning's festivities? It's a gentle color, beautiful, but has a hint of royalty as well. What do you think?" She holds a dress up to my shoulders. It's silky, covered in pearls and jewels and bits of lace around the wrists and neck. It is beautiful and elegant and heavy and, she's right, royal.

I think of the yellow clip Runa gave me the other day. The outfits she's been trying to get me to wear lately—floofy skirts and Taylor Swift T-shirts and baggy jean jackets—aren't anything like these gowns, but they're just as impossible to imagine actually wearing.

"What's today?" I ask.

"A speech," Lady Genevive says. I can tell the other girls don't want to have to tell me anything, which means it must be bad news. "A speech in town assuring the kingdom that you are prepared. That you're a true princess now. That the dragons will leave us soon. People are—well, they're frightened. And yesterday was . . . unnerving. So they need to know that you will take care of them."

"Me?"

"*The Tale of Dragons True* is very clear about what happens when a princess turns twelve, as you know."

"The tale of what?" I ask, my throat suddenly dry. My legs turn to mush.

"*The Tale of Dragons True.*" Lady Genevive emits a sigh that seems to come all the way from her toes to her lips. "Do you need to rest more? This is serious, Princess Auden, and you don't seem very serious right now." She sounds like a person trying not to be annoyed. I know because it's the way Runa has been sounding about me lately, too, and I hate it.

"No, I know, I just—*The Tale of Dragons True*? You, like, have that here?" The words almost get lost in the swarm of feelings. *My book!* I'm suddenly shy and excited, shaky at the idea of my and Runa's stories being seen by other people. My brain can't force it all to make sense. The impossibility has me panicked and proud.

Lady Genevive's whole face scrunches in confusion and unscrunches in frustration. "Don't be absurd," she says.

She goes to the tall bookshelf that is mostly home to tiaras and golden hairbrushes and glass dishes filled with twinkling jewels. And a book. I hadn't noticed it, but Lady Genevive grabs it, puts it in my hands.

"You know it's always nearby. For moments like this, I suppose. If you need to meet with my father so he can help you understand it, I can get him for you."

The Tale of Dragons True the book says on its brown, worn cover. It is not the journal Runa and I wrote in. But is not *not* the journal. It's the same size and shape, the same color. It feels the same in my hands, but instead of the title being written in pink highlighter on the first page, it is embossed in gold on the cover. And when I open it up, I don't see our handwriting, but I see our words, in a ridiculously curvy cursive. And the drawings—the drawings are the very ones Runa and I made. Our renderings of dragons. Our maps of kingdoms. Our etchings of smoke and flames and castles with too many towers.

Sorrowfeld is a kingdom unlike any other, it reads, the words we wrote when we were seven and playing with old dresses my mother had discarded and that we'd imagined into princess gowns: a red sundress with ribbon straps, a silky pink one with long sleeves that Mom wore to a friend's wedding. We'd piled necklaces around our necks, plastic tiaras in our hair. I wish those littler versions of us could see the real thing here, now. *There are three princesses in Sorrowfeld*, we wrote, then later when we outgrew princesses, we revised it to one single princess. *As beautiful as beautiful can be*, we'd said. I can't remember who wrote what, exactly. Back then, we had the same ideas, we'd built Sorrowfeld together the way we used blocks when we were even smaller. One on top of another on top of another until it got so tall it toppled and we had to start over.

We started over again and again and again.

But still, somehow, the book is here. Our *Tale of Dragons True*.

For a forever moment, I can't breathe.

Then I do, and it feels like a hurricane in my mouth.

"This is the book about the rules of the kingdom," I say. I know I sound ridiculous to Genevive, but I can't pretend that this is expected, that it is normal, to find myself in a world I imagined, holding a book I wrote.

I suddenly notice a feather plume in Lady Genevive's hand, and she uses it to scribble on a pad of paper so heavy it seems to be weighing her down. The cover is made of something that looks an awful lot like gold, and the pages are decorated with gold too, from the look I get at them.

I have a flash of Runa and me writing something about golden books and golden pens and golden everything when we were eight or nine and wanted Sorrowfeld to be as fancy as possible. It looks awkward in real life. Heavy. Hard.

A thousand things we wrote rush into my head. We were so silly and so reckless and so giggly and so, so, so not thinking any of it could ever be real.

My head hurts.

"I should get my father," Lady Genevive says. "He can help you. He knows which parts mean what, he is the expert." Lady Genevive exchanges glances with the other girls in the room. They are looks of worry, looks of wondering if maybe this is a sign that I am not a true princess after all.

But thinking of getting Duke Verden makes me smile. He thinks of himself as an expert on the book I've been writing my whole life.

"I don't need help," I say, trying to match her annoyance. I didn't come all the way to the kingdom of

Sorrowfeld to bother someone who looks just like my best friend. I could do that in Magnolia Bend. "I can look at it myself."

"On your own?" one of the girls interrupts, then covers her own mouth, shutting herself up.

"For a refresher," I say. "Just, like, to remember the basics."

There's a large, deep pause. It is oceanic.

"You're meant to work with Duke Verden to interpret it. The enchanted text has been changing quite a bit lately, and you need him to help you understand what is real and what is the witch trying to confuse us, what is a trick. I'll go get him."

I shake my head to stop her talking. It's too much information to try to work through at once. They call it an enchanted text. It changes all the time—of course it does—Runa and I change it constantly, focusing on new ideas, scribbling out what seems, according to her, babyish.

I guess if the text changes depending on what Runa and I are doing in the regular world, that sort of means . . . we are the ones enchanting it?

For a moment, there's a sparkle of something in my chest. Magic. All along we've been practicing magic.

Then the girl with the periwinkle gown rolls her eyes the way Emily always does, and the sparkle dims, disappears, and I'm not a secret enchantress at all. I'm what I've always been—a girl out of her depth, who doesn't know the rules, who isn't doing things quite the right way.

I try to find my way back to being a princess. "Aren't there stories of dragons and how they're actually sad and they used to be humans and now they're—"

"Princess Auden," Lady Genevive interrupts. I didn't know she was allowed to interrupt me, and I don't think she knew that either. "The witch wrote that. Obviously. It's not to be trusted."

"Why would you think a witch wrote just that one part?"

"Enchanted texts are delicate things. Susceptible to manipulation. The recent chapters that have appeared about dragons as some sort of victims? As creatures we should pity? You know we don't look at those pages. They're dangerous. Reading them could put you under their spell. Duke Verden has been very clear on that. You haven't been reading the radical pages, have you? That's not why you're struggling, is it?" Princess Genevive looks genuinely worried, even her neck straining with stress.

I've heard people be scared of certain books before. They show up at our school library sometimes and take away stories we love, certain that they're bad for us. My stomach is squiggly at the idea of that happening here, too, to the stories Runa and I have spent days upon days writing.

But Lady Genevive needs me to say I haven't looked, so I say I haven't looked. Maybe those pages mean something different here. Maybe Runa and I did something dangerous, even, by accident, in writing them. If we'd known we were writing a real place, we would have taken more care, scribbled less, been more thoughtful about what to put in and what to take out. Our *Tale of Dragons True* is sprawling and messy and contradictory and silly. We should have been more serious.

"Well. Good. You haven't done anything dangerous. Let's get you dressed," Genevive says. She helps me take off the nightgown I've been wearing and pulls the gown over what seems to be some sort of little slip. I don't remember putting any of these garments on, but here they are, all old-fashioned and elaborate and slinky-smooth.

The gown is as heavy as I expected, but so beautiful it takes my breath away. It fits me perfectly. In my regular clothes, I'm a kid—all bruised knees and arms that don't know where to go and this sort of ache in my chest, lately, like a warning that it's going to change shape. I've been missing the way I used to feel when

Runa and I did things like jump off the high rock into the river, or practice cartwheels on the lawn at school, or run after the ice cream truck so fast and so hard that we'd collapse in front of it when it finally stopped. In Magnolia Bend, I've been misjudging where my shoulders are in relationship to the doorframes. I've been tripping over my feet, which seem to be squeezing out of my favorite sneakers. I've been annoyed at the way sweatshirts and jeans and my best, most worn T-shirts feel lately. Tight in some places and loose in others and awkward everywhere, like they never even belonged to me.

This dress doesn't feel like that, even though it most certainly does not belong to me.

It fits the way my favorite red-striped sweater used to fit. It fits comfortably and easily, the waist not too tight, the skirt not too long, the sleeves so easy to slip on I could forget there are sleeves at all. Lady Genevive holds up a mirror to me, and I look beautiful.

I look like a princess.

I have the costume and the set. I know this world; I invented it. I can play this part. I don't have to be Denny, who is always one step behind. I can play the part of Princess Auden, who knows what she's doing.

"A speech," I say. "To convince them I can save the kingdom."

"Because you can," Lady Genevive says.

"Because you have to," the girl in charge of the periwinkle dress says.

In the distance, there is a sound like the hoot of an owl, but longer, harder, worse.

I know enough about dragons to know exactly what it is.

Chapter 15

Denny Greene

Runa and I did not include princess speeches in our writings about the history of dragons. We wrote at first about their balls, their romances, their crystal shoes, their castle towers. We drew pictures of their crowns, then maps of their castles, of the kingdom as a whole. We sprinkled magic into a million corners—talking fish and mermaid gatherings and fairies flying around. Ice that turned into diamonds. Flowers that made you fall in love.

But I wonder if we ever even had them speak, our princesses. We could have written anything. But we didn't write much about the young girls in the castles after the first year or two of Sorrowfeld. Lately, we've only cared about the tragic beasts who tortured them.

The things that hurt and worried and baffled them. It feels unfair that I couldn't have visited Sorrowfeld when I was eight and we hadn't turned everything so threatening and strange. There would have been more balls. More fairies. More crystal.

My throat tightens. That's mostly gone now. Here and at home, too.

And now I have to write the rest of the story we started: what a princess says when she is the only one who can save her people.

I've never saved anyone. Except when I saved my mom by being born. But since then, I haven't been able to do much saving at all.

But here I'm not Denny. I'm Princess Auden. And Runa wrote that twelve-year-old princesses are special, so maybe I am.

Maybe I really might be. I try to let the hope of it course through me. It feels sort of new and a little great, as well.

Lady Genevive and I ride in a carriage made of rubies and crystal and gold all the way to the center of town. The wheels are heavy silver, shockingly shiny for something that runs through dirt and grass and thumps across cobblestones. The woman driving us is dressed in heavy brown material and white gloves. She has an elaborate top hat and a straight back, and she doesn't look at us once. Lady Genevive acts like she's not there at all, but I say hello. She nods in response.

"Mother says you just need to be strong and sure," Lady Genevive says. "Let them know you can handle it. You don't need to say much. They just need to believe you."

I nod. I know a little about pretending to be strong, telling everyone I can handle it.

The carriage bumps and jiggles. Lady Genevive keeps reaching around to adjust my hair and my stole and my tiara, even though it's all so tightly in place we'd have to be swept up in a tornado for them to shift.

"What happens if I can't show them how strong I am?" I ask. Runa was like this too, sometimes, telling me things in vague terms instead of concrete ones. Letting me know I had to do something, but never really telling me what exactly it was. Just giving me hair clips and advice on what jeans to buy, but never telling me that next thing—what would happen if I couldn't be a person who fit those things.

"If you don't defeat the dragons, another kingdom will step in. Another princess. And then Sorrowfeld will be theirs. You know all this. It's what your parents worked so hard for, Princess Auden. It's what they died for. Saving the kingdom. From dragons but also from the other rulers in other places who can take advantage of a kingdom without a princess."

It's a familiar story. I wrote it last year, when Runa's hair and legs got longer. When she started texting Sadie with the shiny new phone her parents got her. I wrote about princesses taking over, ousting other princesses who weren't good enough. I wrote about the princesses left behind, who weren't princesses anymore. Who weren't anyone, really.

"Right," I say. "Of course. Other princesses."

We're approaching the town square now, I'm sure of it. There is more jostling inside the carriage and more noise outside. People are gathered, holding bouquets of flowers and looking up at the sky. I think they're expecting the dragons to return, to battle me, to finish what they started. The idea is terrifying, and I'm a breath away from telling Lady Genevive the truth about who I am, but the carriage slows and the driver in the top hat opens the door for me and I can finally see the rest of Sorrowfeld.

And it's beautiful. The town is quiet and sweet, made up of cobblestone pathways that cut through sunflower patches. There are thatch-roof cottages and fruit trees. There are vines on the buildings and daisies in the grass and birds flying everywhere—blue ones mostly, a few red cardinals and tiny, furious-winged hummingbirds too.

I smile at the sunflowers, Runa's favorite flowers, and plum trees, my favorite fruit. The kingdom is filled with colors and shapes and smells we love, things that made us feel safe or excited or alive. It's ours, but it's the villagers' too—a world come alive with the exact ways they planted their gardens, the heights of their homes, the curves in the paths, the way they hold their bodies, smile, worry.

The driver holds her hand out to me, and I step onto a crystal stool and am led up into a golden gazebo with an ornate pedestal that is clearly only there for me. The whole town of Sorrowfeld appears to be waiting for me. I don't recognize any of them from yesterday; I was too startled by the dragon and my imaginary world come to life to worry about who was who. The women wear their hair back in tight little braids, and the men have beards like my dad. They're all in sturdy boots, comfortable jackets. They are strangers and also so familiar, I get dizzy.

"Hello," I say. "Good morning, um, everyone." I sound like my principal when she's giving a speech about how long our skirts have to be or reminding us to be kind to new students. I do not sound like a princess.

I try again, focusing on the fit of the dress, the weight of the crown, the way the castle is visible in the distance. *I am Princess Auden*, I say in my head, the way I was planning to say *I am Dorothy Gale* in my head before my *Wizard of Oz* audition. I was going to wear a blue-and-white-checkered dress. I was going to have braids. I was going to walk into the auditorium as Dorothy, and not give myself a chance to mess it up as Denny.

Denny messes this kind of thing up.

But I am not Denny here. And this isn't Magnolia Bend. This is a place I know. This is a place I made. I am a princess in a land I wrote into being. I can do this. I pull my shoulders back and pretend I am lifting a pen to the page, pretend I am writing things the way I wish they would be, instead of the way they are. And from that place, I find a voice that is befitting a princess.

"Citizens of Sorrowfeld, thank you for being here. It is always an honor to be in the village of Sorrowfeld, a welcome retreat from the palace." The words come more easily than I would have thought, like an improv exercise we did last summer when I was brave enough to go to theater camp for a week.

Like a monologue I deliver about how my mom likes gardening and classical music when someone asks about my family, even though for the last year she's let the garden grow wild, the house fall silent.

"I know we are all scared—frightened—by the dragons." I pause and look at their faces to understand how they feel about dragons. They stare at the ground, stealing glimpses at the sky, like if they glance upward too long, the dragons will come out and burn down the town. "But I'm a princess. And now I'm twelve." The words aren't much, but I say them squarely, assuredly. I straighten my back even more. I try a smile that is small but steady. "I am Princess Auden of Sorrowfeld," I say, "and I will save the kingdom."

I take a step back from the podium, so they know I'm done speaking. It was almost nothing, what I said, but I said it like I was unafraid and royal, and I guess that's all they need, because they begin to clap, then cheer, and then someone starts playing a flute and someone else a fiddle, and there is dancing in the town square, lifted knees and swinging arms and mouths that are open and singing and shouting out thank-yous to me.

It was enough; whatever I did, it was enough.

Lady Genevive and I are both led back into the carriage, and for a few moments, I feel like Princess Auden. As if I have already saved the kingdom.

"I'm so glad you turned true," Lady Genevive says. "When you defeat the dragons, there will be a huge celebration. I can't wait. Do you think they'll come back soon to battle?" She seems so sure it will all work out, just from the words I said and the way I said them.

Then there it is. A feeling I know well—the feeling that comes after you have spun a tale you wish were true. The moment I open the door to my house and call out hello to someone who doesn't answer. How sour and wrong it feels, to pretend my mother is still the person she used to be.

The truth is heavy when it reminds you it's there.

There's a rock in my stomach, a boulder of a thing that doesn't know how to fix this. "I couldn't even save my mother," I say to Lady Genevive.

"You were only three," Lady Genevive says. "No one could save her."

She's talking about Princess Auden's mother, of course.

But that's not who I meant.

I can wear princess gowns and say royal words and pretend to be someone I have never been. But I don't know how to battle a dragon or save anyone at all. Dad's told me that Mom's favorite thing is being a mother. He's said that spending time with me will help her. That she got better because I was born, and now I'm here and she'll remember to get better again.

But she's only ever gotten worse.

"I only make things worse," I say, wishing it was enough to make Lady Genevive truly understand me, but of course it isn't.

Chapter 16

Denny Greene

"She did really well," Lady Genevive reports to her parents over dinner. We are eating on a balcony off one of the turrets, bowls of grapes and kiwis and piles of cheese everywhere. There are sweet drinks in silver goblets and breads so fluffy I kind of want to fall asleep on them.

I get a flicker of feeling about home. Dad cooks dinners that are always warm and rich and comfortable—like if he makes something cozy enough to eat, Mom might actually come downstairs to have it with us. So there are always bowls of mac and cheese and dishes of lasagna and so many soups—potato, tomato, wild rice, squash. On the weekends he bakes bread. He always picks up scones from our favorite bakery. The house usually smells delicious—cinnamon and pumpkin spice, or onions and garlic and melting cheese.

I like these fruits and fluffy breads at the castle, but Dad would grumble about them if he was told they were dinner.

"That's wonderful. See? You can do this, Princess Auden," Duke Verden says. He has a very definitive way of speaking, every word heavy and firm. "You'll defeat the dragons and then we can all move forward. You and I can figure out what our kingdom needs next. With that threat taken care of at last, there will be so many other things for us to do. The kingdom is counting on us."

I prickle a little. Runa and I did not invent Sorrowfeld so that some random duke older than our dads could be in charge. She'd hate the way he keeps saying he knows how to interpret our words, as if somehow he's closer to them than we are.

"I'm trying. I don't know exactly what to do next, but I'm trying," I say. I shiver. It's a little cold out here, but the sky is exactly the way Runa and I wrote it: absolutely smothered in stars. I'd do anything to be able to show it to Runa. I miss her all the way down to my toes.

"Well, I'm here to guide you, Princess Auden," Duke Verden says. "I know without a doubt we need the dragons defeated. And we need them defeated *now*. It's imperative we do it quickly. We don't have time to waste."

I try to remember what we've written in *The Tale of Dragons True* that would make Duke Verden so sure speed is important, that now is the time. Runa's insistence that princesses turning twelve means something vital and huge is there, of course, but Duke Verden seems nervous, urgent. I can't quite put my finger on why. And he doesn't give me a chance to ask anything else.

"We need the kingdom to have trust in you, and we need you, Princess Auden, to trust in yourself. You can save us. And it sounds like you did an excellent job today."

Duchess Dutton nods and piles persimmons onto my plate. "Your parents would be proud," she says.

I try to smile at the compliment, but I know *my* parents would not be proud. They would be furious that I'm here at all. They'd say I need to be home with them. Mom would slump around saying she's doing her best and why isn't that enough for me? Dad would say we have to work together as a family to get Mom back on track, so I need to stay close. Only Runa would feel proud. Old Runa, who liked dragons even more than me, who fell asleep once in our garden shed because she was so engrossed in a story she was writing that she forgot to go home, and we all spent hours looking for her, worried about her, only to find her snoring under the fairy lights, clutching *The Tale of Dragons True* like it was a blankie.

New Runa would probably say that princesses are for babies and that Sadie would have done a better job talking to the kingdom. And maybe she'd be right.

I don't think I like persimmons very much. And I definitely don't like the soft blue cheese Duchess Dutton has spread onto the pillow-bread for me. I can't settle into this world—it's the place I built, and it's also something else, filled with unexpected details that seem to have shimmied their way in. I like the turrets and tiaras, and I felt overcome by the dragons—in awe of their size and shape and realness. But there is so much we never would have written in—tastes and smells and tones of voice I hate.

It feels so unfair that even the place I imagined isn't right. That actually I don't fit in anywhere. They're all smiling at me, forks clinking, nerves calming. But my insides twist as I realize I'm all wrong and misfitting in Sorrowfeld too.

"I don't think I'm really—" I start, but before the whole sentence can come out, there is the flapping of wings. The darkening of sky.

They're distant, but they stop us all anyway. We put down forks and napkins and pieces of papaya. We look up to the sky, all of us at once. The air warms, slightly, but I'm goose bumping like crazy. Duchess Dutton puts her hand by her throat. Lady Genevive scoots closer to me. Duke Verden stands up, like he's ready to do battle himself, even though I have heard no one say that a duke can do much of anything to save a kingdom. He is all straight-backed and steely-eyed, looking into the starry night at the dragon, which is closer now, louder, the bright orange of its nostrils visible before the rest of it. Three others following in the distance.

I think I'm supposed to stand too, but I don't, I can't. It's not fear exactly, but shock, startle, maybe even a sort of pride at how magnificent they truly are, off the page. I had hoped we'd thought up a creature that was brave and strong and undeniable, and we really, really did. And it's right here, looking at me.

I don't want to defeat the dragons, I think, but somehow have the wherewithal not to say. I don't want them to hurt me, of course, but I don't want them to vanish. I spent years making them up. I don't want to extinguish them now, when they're actually real.

"Is it now?" I ask. "Do I have to do this now?"

No one replies. Duchess Dutton grips the table. I

hear a clattering of plates, a flurry of doors and screams inside the castle. But the four of us stay right where we are, like we're keeping a promise we didn't know we'd made.

The dragon is above us now. She's green and gray and mean-faced, the others behind her flying in swoops and circles. Menacing. This one dives toward us, then back up, and I don't know what to do, except that Duchess Dutton keeps begging me to do something, something, something. "Princess Auden, please," she says. "Princess Auden, save us." I stand next to Duke Verden, even though the whole of me wants to disappear under the table or to join the dragons in the sky.

It's weird, how I want both at once.

"What do princesses do?" I ask. "I don't know how princesses defeat dragons." I'm speaking quickly and quietly and urgently, and my hands find his arm and grip it the way a bird attaches to a branch. He is so strong, he is so sure and stately. I don't know much about him, except that he is beloved and courageous and that he knows things about the kingdom of Sorrowfeld that I clearly, somehow, do not. "Please help me," I say, right in time with Duchess Dutton pleading for me to be the one to help.

"Only a princess knows," Duke Verden says, his voice frustrated, exasperated. He looks right at me. His eyes are blue and wide, he is running his hands through his hair, taking tight breaths. "This is what you have to do. The book says. It's time. It's time!" He's yelling now, shaking a hand above his head like it might summon my abilities.

I swallow and close my eyes and hope for a way to know what to do. All I can hear is the flapping of wings and Duke Verden's desperate voice.

The dragon flies closer, smoke filling the air, almost choking me, the thickness and smell of it making it hard to breathe. Everyone believes that I can somehow put a stop to this beast, but I can't and I don't and I'm not and oh my *gosh* they are here, they are on us, their skin so scaly and thick and beautiful, their size impossible.

And then.
Whoosh.
Whap.
Flame.
Flap.

We're in a cloud of smoke, I've been pushed to the ground by the force of the dragons, the air hot and heavy, and there is a scream so loud and deep and all kinds of wrong, but it takes until the smoke clears to understand who it is from.

Duke Verden.

He is in the dragon's claws, his body being lifted up and away from us. The wings of the dragon are hurricane strong, and the duke is what seems like miles above us before we even have a chance to know it is him and that he has been taken.

My hands grip my shoulders. I never would have written a story like this.

"No!" Duchess Dutton cries. "No! No!" She waves her hands. She jumps, a pointless gesture that would be funny if it weren't so awful, so desperate and sad. Lady Genevive begins to cry, her breathing in a race with my heartbeat, and both of them winning. And I shake, every part of me—fingers and toes, knocking knees, shoulders that shiver and a chin that wobbles itself back and forth, back and forth.

The dragon is gone, and Duke Verden with her, and it is an impossible and terrible thing, it is maybe the worst thing I have ever seen, and I have seen my mother refuse to come downstairs for Christmas, and I have seen my father cry at two in the morning outside his bedroom door when he thinks I'm sleeping.

We listen to the dragon flap away, farther and farther, until the sound of her wings is no louder than a heartbeat, and then is quieter still, until it is nothing, just an echo in our ears of the worst thing that has ever happened.

"I'm sorry," I say, in the dust that has been dragged up and the smoke that stings our eyes. "I'm so sorry."

"They didn't kill him," Duchess Dutton says. Her voice is edgy and strained. "They didn't kill him, so we can get him back. You can get him back. Sometimes a dragon takes someone, as part of battle, and a princess fights back, and that's what you have to do, Princess Auden. You have to do it now."

"I don't— I can't— The dragon was here, and I didn't know what to do, there wasn't some sudden princess magic that—"

"You are twelve." Duchess Dutton's voice shifts into something new. It is loud and angry. Exasperated. "You are not a child, you can stop whining and you can fix it. You can do what princesses do." She doesn't look at me as she speaks. I can see it is hard for her to get a full breath in, hard for her to stand at all. She hangs her head, like those few sentences took everything out of her and all that's left is just one single whispered word that breaks my heart.

"Please."

The Tale of Dragons True

Runa, age 11

The dragons get braver, once a princess turns twelve. They know she is more powerful, so they are more powerful too. They are scary, but they are fair.

Dragons are always fair.

Chapter 17

Princess Auden

I stay up most of the night looking through this girl Denny's worldly possessions. Her room is quite odd—there are shiny polka dots on the walls and piles of stiff, strange clothing on the floor. Most unsettling, however, is a collection of dragon-shaped objects on a shelf in her room and piled on her bed. Perhaps she's a dragon tamer of some kind, and when she captures the terrible beings, she is able to shrink them down and make them immobile? Perhaps she is an artist, crafting dragon goods. But who would they be for? The dragons themselves?

I've never heard of a kingdom such as this one—messy and cluttered and using a strange, meandering form of English I'm not familiar with. It's an odd dialect that sounds rude in practice. And both her parents have rectangular magical devices that they get lost in midsentence.

Sorcery, I assume, but I thought most of the magic was in forest lands, and this place is green yards and square homes and carriages made of metal with no horses.

There are extremely realistic paintings of a girl who looks just like me, except wearing the odd clothing of this kingdom. She must be Denny. She's in a variety of locations and poses with her mother and father and some other acquaintances—lords and ladies, I imagine?—all over her room, in frames. She looks happy in these paintings. Or I look happy. It's odd—this girl is not me. But she is a copy of me, from the shade of her hair to the crinkle of her eyes, and when I pick up one painting where she is in what must be her underclothes at the ocean, I can see her shoulder. I nearly drop the painting.

Her shoulder is my shoulder. Right on the boniest part is a small birthmark in the shape of a heart. I move aside the soft gray fabric of the top I'm wearing because it seems as though perhaps she's stolen it from me—this little detail of my skin that I've been told my mother used to call my *outside heart*. I've always thought of it that way too, a little piece of me that is visible, when so much of who I am has to be locked inside.

I could not possibly count the number of times Duchess Dutton has reminded me to stay *composed*, which is another way of saying cold or removed. The gowns I wear don't show anyone my shoulders, so even my outside heart has always been a hidden one. For a moment, I'm jealous of this Denny, who wears underclothes to visit the ocean, who in other paintings is in dresses or tops where her outside heart is visible too. I'm jealous of the way she smiles in these paintings—like she might lose control of the smile at any moment, like if she is not careful—and she's *not* careful, I can tell—her smile might leap right off her face and away to glow somewhere even better and brighter.

Denny's inside heart gets to show too.

My outside heart is still in its place, and I'm growing tired, so I curl onto Denny's bed, which is narrow and hard and filled with these strange, soft dragon dolls. I take them off the bed and try to bury them underneath. Until I know what they are, I don't want them watching me.

All this feels like the machinations of witches, who have perhaps ordered dragons to kidnap me and bring me here to leave my kingdom unprotected. I remember the dragons coming to my birthday. I remember having no idea what to do, knowing that I was still myself—good at looking the part but not actually made for anything royal. And then there's a blank space before I appeared in this new kingdom. That blank space could be filled by dragons, surely. I drift off to sleep thinking of them.

When I wake up, I'm sure the dragons are here in this home with me. There's the smell of smoke and someone yelling something fearful and urgent, and I rush downstairs and there is Denny's father, upon a chair, waving a towel in front of a beeping device in the ceiling. I was right; there is smoke filling the house, but the smoke is coming from the stovetop. There looks to be a scramble of eggs and peppers in a pan, but they have all been browned into something dry and burnt.

I run to the kitchen windows and open them wide, letting the smoke escape. We know what to do about smoke in Sorrowfeld, but Denny's father looks utterly baffled by the smoke here now.

"It's smoke," I tell him. "From fire. Perhaps you cooked this meal for a bit too long?"

"Denny, I know what smoke is," he replies, sounding tired and irritated, but his limbs are flailing and his cheeks are pink and he has not called in anyone to assist him.

"Did the chef make a mistake?" I ask.

"Is that what you're calling Mom now?"

I look around for the mother, but she's not here.

It's barely seven in the morning, and I'm tired already, trying to piece together the mysterious rules of this home, this kingdom.

"She made this?" I ask. "Is it a meal for the family?"

"I don't know what she was thinking, she knows you hate everything but cereal and I'm not a breakfast person, but I think she felt bad about yesterday maybe, I think she wanted to try to make something right, but, I don't know, Den, I guess she just took on more than she was ready for right now. But she tried. That's something, Denny. She tried."

I nod but I don't understand, and he is so on edge I can't ask questions. The smell is awful and the mom is nowhere to be seen and he pours me a bowl of something flaky and beige, which he then covers in milk.

"Porridge?" I ask.

"Denny, are you not feeling well? Or is this some sort of method acting for your audition? Did Dorothy not know what Frosted Flakes were?"

Answering seems like it will just open up more confusion, so I don't answer and spoon the strange, hard porridge into my mouth. It explodes with sweetness there. It is decadent and light at once, crunchy but softening quickly in the milk. And so, so sweet. A new kind of sweet I don't recognize.

"This is marvelous," I say. I have liked almost nothing

about this new kingdom, but this burst of flavor and texture is exceptional, and for a moment I forget about where I am not and let myself just be where I am.

The father chuckles and wishes me luck—on what I don't know—but soon he is telling me to hurry, that the bus is coming, that I'm going to be late, that he can't take me in because clearly Mom can't be alone right now, and to please be home early because Mom misses me.

This comment makes no sense at all. I miss a mother who is *actually* gone. That's what missing is. Why does this mother miss Denny when she is right upstairs, always hiding away, and could just come down and see her? A little flurry of anger shakes around in my chest, and I try to quiet it and instead focus on organizing his words into rules, but it's hard. I'm supposed to move fast, I'm supposed to come home early, I'm supposed to do something with the mother, I'm supposed to not ask too many questions.

I don't think I'm a princess in this world. No one bows to me. No one asks me my preferences.

No one is listening to me at all, really.

A bit of calm washes over me. I'm not in charge. I'm not important. If I just follow the rules here, surely that will be good enough.

Maybe I will finally, finally be good enough for who I am meant to be.

Without another word or instruction or reminder to straighten my back or live up to my title, the father opens the door, throws a heavy bag across my shoulders, and a yellow carriage arrives in front of the home. It is a loud, strange vehicle, and smoke is coming out of it too. It does seem that perhaps it is the work of dragons—that this is a kingdom filled with smoke. The carriage—what the father called the bus—is filled with children of all ages, and they are loud, they are in shiny clothing, their hair is undone, as if they stopped in the middle of getting ready.

One such child calls to me. "Denny, over here!" and I follow the sound of her voice while the bus startles away from the home. To where, I don't know.

I look at the girl who called me over, and my heart darts up to my throat. It is Lady Genevive! Except it is also not.

"You're here too?" I say, scooching close to her. She's in the clothing of this new kingdom—stiff pants and a shiny shirt and a heavy parcel in bright colors carried on her back.

"Of course I'm here," she says, and her voice has the tenor of Lady Genevive's, but not the pattern. "You look weird."

"I do?"

"Weren't you wearing that yesterday? At your party? And it's all, like, wrinkled."

"No one came to dress me," I whisper, realizing it for the first time myself.

Her face scrunches. It is not an expression Lady Genevive makes. In fact, it is not Lady Genevive's face. So much is the same, but there's an essential *something* missing—a quality that makes Lady Genevive her own self and not, well, whoever this is. "Are you sick?" she asks. "Like, do you have a fever?" She puts a hand upon my forehead. The feeling is cool and friendly and then she shrugs, unable to tell, I guess. "You can't miss school, it's auditions. Get it together, okay? Don't be weird."

This is not Lady Genevive.

And I am not Denny, but I think I have to try to be Denny as best I can. I don't know who Denny is, but she looks just like me and we share the same heart on our shoulder, so I need to do right by her.

Pretending to be Denny cannot possibly be harder than pretending to be a worthy princess.

"I shall not be weird," I say, and this girl cringes.

"Runa!" Another girl enters the bus and comes straight for us. She sits in the seat in front of us, immediately turning to face us. "Oh, and hi, Denny," she says, but it's clear I'm not the main event here. It's a strange feeling. When I'm with Lady Genevive, no one is ever clamoring for her. They are curtsying to me, waving to me, beaming when I so much as glance at them. Here, even my own mother shuts herself away in a tower far from me. "I almost missed the bus, I was trying to get my hair right, and it just would not cooperate, do you have extra clips?"

"Hey, Sadie! I've got extras," Runa says, handing this girl three sparkly purple clips. "Excited for today?" Runa sits up on her knees, so I do the same.

"Hi, Sadie," I try.

Sadie blinks. Scans my clothing. Looks away.

I need to change my own clothes tomorrow. And wear clips. And speak in some different tone of voice.

"SO excited," Sadie says, mostly to Runa. "I sounded good yesterday, right? I think I'm gonna get it."

"You sounded great!" Runa says, before looking at me. "Sorry, after we went bowling yesterday, we helped Sadie with her audition. I would have helped you but, you know, you sort of had a lot going on."

"But of course," I say. Being in this new kingdom is like being a detective, trying to piece together an order of events that somehow got us all here, on this bus that smells a little sweet and a little sweaty.

"Yeah, sorry, but, like, that wasn't really a party, you know?" Sadie asks. She has a wrinkle in her nose and still hasn't really looked me in the eyes. Her gaze hits somewhere around the top of my head, where usually my crown would be. For a moment, I miss it.

"Yes. No. Not a party. Of course not."

Duchess Dutton taught me the importance of being agreeable. When I talk to the villagers, she says the most important thing is to be a leader and the second most important thing is to be an agreeable leader. An agreeable leader nods a lot and listens and says *yes yes yes*, even if they're not actually going to do what the person is asking for.

I must have looked confused, because Duke Verden broke in. "You do what you need to do later, when they're not watching," he said, like it was the obvious answer.

After a few more stops picking up other children who squeal or whine or laugh or stay quiet with their shoulders hunched over heavy books, we make a final stop where everyone seems to be getting off. I give Runa and Sadie a quick glance and get off as well.

"So, we have arrived at our destination," I say.

Runa elbows me. "Stop being weird," she says. "Everyone's going to notice."

Usually, being noticed is a good thing. Duchess Dutton says a princess should not blend in; she should stand out. Duchess Dutton says all of Sorrowfeld should know when I have walked into a room. Duchess Dutton says I am the most important person in the kingdom, and I need to act like it.

But I'm also supposed to be agreeable.

And then do what I need to do behind their backs.

The rules contradict each other sometimes. And I'm the only one who seems to notice that.

I look up at the large brick building in front of me. Maybe here, the rules are easier to follow.

Chapter 18

Princess Auden

All day long we sit at desks and listen to teachers in scratchy sweaters with scratchier voices. Everything about it is hard. The lessons themselves, yes, filled with questions I don't know the answers to, histories I've never studied, mathematical equations no one has ever required a princess to know.

I learned to read, of course, from my tutors. And I took waltzing lessons and the flute. I learned the painting of still lifes and which crowns go with which gowns. I spent many months memorizing the neighboring kingdoms and the names of the princesses there, in case we ever needed to call upon them for help.

And I learned about dragons—what sorts of

climates they prefer, the foods they eat, the kingdoms they have enflamed.

These teachers do not speak of dragons, though. Or princesses, kingdoms, castles, or gowns. And when they call on me to answer questions—which they seem to do whether or not I have given any indication that I might know the answer—I try to explain this to them.

"I require more instruction on this topic," I say to one teacher with curly brown hair and freckles. "Shall we schedule a time?"

"*This* is the time, Denny," the teacher says, a mild irritation polluting her voice.

"I thought perhaps some private instruction might be useful." I'm unbothered by mild irritation. Duke Verden's voice is loud and booming when he's upset, which is often. Duchess Dutton does everything I ask but almost always with something that looks like an eye roll. Dragons visit me on every birthday. I am tolerated by the people I live with, not loved.

Aside from Lady Genevive, who I miss desperately as I listen to the snickering of the other children in class with me.

"Do you need a trip to the principal's office, Denny?" the teacher asks, her irritation growing far past mild.

"I don't know, do I?" I ask, but it must come out incorrectly, because the teacher's eyes go wide, and she purses her lips like she's trying to keep something bad from coming out of them.

"Last chance. Pull yourself together. This is a classroom, not a comedy routine."

Everyone in class is smirking, and I don't know how to right the moment, so I go quiet and still, which is one of the things *The Tale of Dragons True* says to do when surprised by a dragon. Go still. Go quiet. Dragons are so emotional and out of control they can miss you, if you blend into the background.

The teacher is not a dragon. It works anyway, at least for the remainder of the day. But it won't work forever. I need to understand how to behave here. I don't know what a principal is, but it sounds dangerous, serious. I don't want a visit to a principal; I don't know what kinds of cruel punishments exist in this world if you don't follow the rules. It's uncomfortable being this unknown, unknowing person in this unknown, unknowable world.

A bell that has been ringing all day chimes extra long, extra awful, and it sets everyone in motion. Packing parcels. Shoving heavy books and broken pencils inside, strapping the monstrosities onto their backs.

"It's okay if you can't do it," Runa says in the rush.

"Can't do it?" I have taken to repeating everything

everyone says, because I don't know how to respond to much of what they are saying to me.

"Like last time. If you just can't get the song out or read the script or whatever. I mean, it's fine. Sadie will be a really good Dorothy, and it's probably easier that way anyway, you know?"

"Easier?"

Something I have noticed about Runa is that she is very nervous, but she is pretending to be very not nervous. I want to tell her it will be okay, whatever it is, but I suppose I don't actually know that to be true.

"I think Sadie would be mad, if you got it," Runa says, speaking carefully, like her voice is on tiptoes. "She doesn't know how good you are. And we're, like, just becoming friends with them, you know? And it's going really well. So maybe it's better if we don't totally make her mad."

I don't want to keep asking Runa questions, but unfortunately she keeps saying things that make no sense at all.

"And you owe me. From the party. And it would just be worse, if you were Dorothy, after all that, you know? Sadie would really not be cool with you then."

Lady Genevive speaks this way too, sometimes, when she is uncertain of her role in things, when she is navigating a disagreement, when I can tell that she would prefer to be outside with regular girls rather than trapped in a tower with me.

"I don't think I quite comprehend," I say, which isn't exactly the same as asking yet another question, but it's close.

"I'm not saying you shouldn't audition. You should audition. Just maybe, like, don't worry about how well you do?"

I don't know what kind of audition Denny is supposed to go to today, but in the kingdom we have auditions for royal entertainers frequently. Clowns for the children's festivals and harpists for New Year's, and singers for solstice. Once, Lady Genevive dared me to put on a disguise and pretend to audition to be one of the solstice singers. I astounded everyone by being chosen, and then revealing myself to be Princess Auden and not, of course, a member of the royal chorus.

We didn't often do things that were sneaky or naughty, Lady Genevive and I, but every once in a great long while, we would make a joke or enact a plan that Duke Verden admonished as childish and unbecoming of a princess but that was, without a doubt, fun. Auditioning was fun. Singing was fun. And being good at singing—well, that was something a little different than fun. I had never been good at something without also being a princess. And when you're a princess, it's hard to know for sure whether you are good or whether you are simply beloved.

I am not beloved in the kingdom of Magnolia Bend. I'm not sure I'm even particularly liked.

But I can sing.

"I'll think about it," I say.

"There are other parts in *The Wizard of Oz*, anyway," Runa goes on. "Maybe you could just be the lion or something? You don't have to be Dorothy. And probably you wouldn't get that part anyway. Probably you'll feel pretty nervous, right?"

It's Runa who looks nervous, and I want to point that out to her, but I get the distinct impression that would not be well received. Duchess Dutton has taught me to always pause before responding, especially when in conversation with those from other kingdoms. It's important to read not just the words they are saying but the thoughts their bodies are indicating.

"Don't worry," I say. "Everything will be as it should be."

"I really like being their friend, Denny," Runa says in a suddenly smaller voice. "I like matching hair accessories and trying makeup and singing along with Emily's playlists. I know it's— I know we don't feel exactly the same about it, and that's kind of—that's weird. But I like being included. I know that doesn't matter as much to you, and you have other bigger stuff to worry about, but when you're off worrying about that and helping your dad and stuff, I'm all alone. Until now. Please don't mess it up for me. Okay?"

I don't know what that means, exactly, or what is so great about being friends with Sadie and Emily, who are sort of aloof and plain. They wear the same clothing as everyone else, and say the same few phrases. They know answers in class, but not every single one, and they have friends, but not more than anyone else. No one has a crown or a title or a bit of magical information, as far as I can tell. No one here can defeat dragons or tell the future or save a kingdom from destruction.

But Runa doesn't seem to know that. To Runa, Sadie and Emily might as well be the princesses of Magnolia Bend.

Or dragons themselves.

Chapter 19

Princess Auden

These auditions are nothing like the ones in Sorrowfeld. There are no thrones, for one, and no aerialists. No one on the fiddle and no mimes. Every single girl in the room sings the same song, for the same amount of time—exactly one minute, and then reads the same few words. The stage is black and dusty, the chairs in the audience are squeaky and red, and a few grown-ups sit in the third row, taking notes on each identical performance.

Runa, Emily, Sadie, and I sit in the back, watching, before it's time for our turns. Runa is going to be designing sets, and Emily is going to be the assistant lighting designer, so they won't be auditioning, but they're watching and making comments on every single girl who goes up there. *She's off pitch. She doesn't* look like a Dorothy. *She was way too dramatic on that line. Is she better than me? Am I better than her? Should I say it that way? They liked that.*

In Sorrowfeld, we keep such things to ourselves. We clap politely for each performer and wait until they are all gone to discuss how they did and who we would like to perform at our festival or celebration. Sadie and Runa and Emily keep looking at me, like I'm supposed to contribute some comments as well, but I don't know what to say so I keep calling each one *Marvelous*, and they keep rolling their eyes like I'm using the wrong word or saying it the wrong way, or am simply just *wrong* in some certain but ineffable way.

When it's Sadie's turn to go, she truly *is* marvelous. Her voice has a way of lifting up and over the audience, like it's something better than the rest of us. And she reads the lines with a seriousness that no one else captured. A few people clap when she's done, even though it does not appear to be traditional to clap after auditions. She floats back to her seat and is greeted by a massive hug from Runa, who tells her she was perfect. I want to tell her the same, but they're calling my name. Or they're calling the name Denny Greene, which sort of belongs to me currently, I suppose.

The stage isn't much like the places I am used to giving speeches or performing songs or flute solos.

Those are all made of silver and are covered in roses and rise up and up and up, far above the villagers. This stage is not too far up from the ground and is dull and scratched up.

"Name?" they ask. In Sorrowfeld—in every kingdom I have ever traveled to—my name is known. I do not introduce myself. I do not have strangers looking at me curiously, wondering who I am, what my talents might be. It's uncomfortable to have to announce oneself, but I do it anyway.

"Auden," I say, before correcting myself. "Denny. Denny Greene." It is so casual, so effortless. The name of someone who could be anyone. I want to keep saying it over and over.

"Okay, Denny, let's see what you've got."

I nod and the girl who has been playing piano for everyone starts the first few notes, and I launch into the song that an hour ago I didn't know, but is now a part of my soul, after having listened to nothing else since entering this theater. I've never sung it before, and the notes surprise me—both the difficulty of them and the way I sound singing them. I try to enjoy the shock of it, the ups and downs and all arounds, the heat of the lights, the dozens of strangers watching me.

It's a song about going somewhere new, and about finding hope there. It's a song about longing for this better place, and when I sing it, it feels like it is a song entirely about me. So I let it be that song, the one about missing my mother and father and sisters, missing the life I never got to live. I let it be a song about what may come true someday—that they could come home, that things could be different, that I could be different. I sing the song about coming here and wondering why, and feeling like I am caught between two places, and those places are Sorrowfeld and Magnolia Bend, but those places are also being a kid princess and being a person who can fix everything, even though I have never fixed anything, ever in my whole life.

I sing it all.

It feels fantastic, like I'm finally breathing and saying something true, and maybe I've never said a true thing in all twelve of my royal years. I'm not Princess Auden. I'm just Denny. I can relax into it. I don't have to try so hard.

When I finish, there is a pause. I can't tell what kind of pause, at first, because it is stretchy and strange and so, so quiet. Then an older kid in the back starts to clap, and others do too. Some of them stand. One of the grown-ups puts her pen down and makes eye contact with me, a slow sort of smile on her face. A girl in the front claps loudest, hardest. She has a loud outfit—bold colors and patterns, and she's wearing what look to be the ears of a cat on a sort of crown affixed to her head. Her face startles me—it is familiar the same way Runa's was familiar. She smiles right at me and I grin back like the two of us have a secret, even though I can't place why her face feels like one I have always known. I am shaky from having sung, from being Dorothy, and from being Denny too.

In Sorrowfeld, I am not supposed to smile so widely, I'm not supposed to enjoy applause so much, but everything is different here, so I hope this is too. I beam and blush and take it in—that I did something special. I wiggle my toes in my sneakers and put my hands in my pockets. I've never had pockets, and it's so lovely, to have a place to store my hands when I don't know what else to do with them.

I read the script words next. They are words about being somewhere new, and missing the place you came from, but wanting to explore this new place as well.

They could be my own words of longing and excitement, of worry and relief. I say them from that same place of wishing and wondering, and they start to feel like they belong to me. This Dorothy person wants to go home, but she also, I think, wants to stay here. She feels like another side of herself, in this new land. She doesn't know why she's been delivered to Oz, but she has to be brave to get through it.

I think I understand Dorothy more than I understand anyone else I have met here. She feels the most familiar, and I sort of snuggle into that as I read her words.

When I'm done, the grown-ups are nodding and chatting amongst themselves. They are tapping a sheet of paper with names on it, and making markings—arrows, stars, it's hard to say from up here.

"Thank you, Denny," the red-haired grown-up with the pencil as sharp as a spindle says. "That was lovely. All of it."

I find my way back to my seat, and I'm not sure what I expect, but the girls are downright icy, especially Sadie, who won't look me in the eye. Runa is the only one who says anything at all.

"Well, you know you did good," she says. She's smiling but sounds sad, and I don't know her well, but it hurts anyway. I know Denny thinks they're friends, but even though I only really know about friends from storybooks and the moat-watching and Lady Genevive, I know this isn't how they are supposed to act.

"It was marvelous," I say, because of how it felt, and because it is the truth.

"Yep," Runa says. The last *p* of the word pops, a sound like opening a bottle of pear petunia fizz, a favorite drink of mine that doesn't seem to be popular in the kingdom of Magnolia Bend.

I've broken another rule, made another misstep. There is no Duke Verden thrusting the enchanted text at me, no Duchess Dutton sighing and making me spend extra hours practicing my fluting or walking with a straight back or curtsying.

In Magnolia Bend, they don't tell me exactly what I have done wrong.

"Is there a book?" I ask Runa quietly. "Of rules? For how to behave?"

Runa looks at me askance "It's not funny, Denny," she says after a thick pause.

"So you just know all the rules by heart?" I ask. This would be harder to figure out, but surely I could do it.

Runa shakes her head *no no no no no* and turns away from me.

Together, but also not really together at all, the four of us watch the rest of the auditions. People are great and terrible. They have loud voices and shaky ones, swoopy and solemn ones. They stumble over the words of the script or read it so passionately there are tears in their eyes.

It doesn't matter who does what, though. None of the girls around me will look at me. No one will talk to me. They exchange glances with one another that are so pointed they are practically touchable.

I try to understand what I've done wrong and why Sadie is allowed to be good but I'm not. Regular Denny would probably have auditioned in the right way that wouldn't have upset anyone.

For a heart-hurting moment, I wish I could be regular Denny. I have always wanted to be regular. I thought I was doing it, but I have to try harder.

"I'm sorry," I say, when auditions are over and Sadie, Emily, Runa, and I are packing up our bags. "I'm really, really sorry."

Runa nods. Emily half smiles.

But Sadie just crosses her arms over her chest and walks away, like I've taken something that belonged to her.

I don't know how to give it back, but I would if I could. Just to be less alone in this cold, busy, noisy kingdom of theirs.

Chapter 20

Princess Auden

I haven't had parents in a long time, but I know they are generally proud of their children. Duchess Dutton is always telling me to make mine proud, as if they might appear one day, ready to assess what it is I have been up to the last eight years. I try, but Duchess Dutton never seems satisfied with those efforts. I keep my back straight and smile at the villagers. I have memorized maps of kingdoms, and I do my best, every birthday, to look unafraid when the dragons appear.

She doesn't like the way I watch regular girls across the moat from my tower. She doesn't like that I keep Lady Genevive in my room later than I'm supposed to, talking about nothing important, ignoring flute and diplomacy and dragon lessons like I don't care about them, which I sometimes sort of don't.

Regular girls, though, aren't as disappointing as princesses who maybe should have been taken by dragons. Their parents clap when they perform silly dances, hug them for the simplest things—curtsying well, sharing their bits of cake, anything, really. I've always wanted that—to do something small and have it mean something big to the people in charge of me.

So I feel a buzz of excitement, coming home, ready to tell Denny's parents about my audition. The cast list hasn't gone up yet of course, but it almost doesn't matter. I want to tell them about the applause, about the way it felt to get lost in Dorothy's words, how hard the song was and how surprised I was when my voice found the path and stayed on it.

"Good evening!" I greet them. They're in the living room, Denny's mother wrapped in a blanket and sipping at something slowly, Denny's father reading a newspaper that he doesn't seem to truly be reading at all. "I auditioned! And it went so well! I think I might even get the part of Dorothy, which I suppose is the part everyone wants. Sadie wants it. Maybe she'll be awarded it. But they all looked at me like I'd done something rather amazing. It was— I wish I could do that every day."

Just like when I was onstage, there's a pause. This one is thicker, though. Harder to move through. And on the other side is just Denny's father, blank-faced and blinking.

"That's a big role," he says. "Are you sure it's a good idea? We have a lot going on here at home."

"Oh. Well. Yes?" I don't have any idea, of course, whether it's a good idea. I don't know what kinds of obligations Denny has, or even what sorts of responsibilities anyone in the kingdom of Magnolia Bend might have. Perhaps they are in a battle with a neighboring kingdom? I should have thought to ask. Perhaps that is why Runa is so tense, why Denny's parents are so quiet and strained. Or Magnolia Bend might have its own threatening beings or magic they are trying to sort out. I have been a bit uncurious about what struggles the kingdom of Magnolia Bend might be confronting, because it's simply such a relief to not hear any talk of dragons or smell their fire or hear their threatening wings.

And besides, it doesn't seem like Denny has all that much to do but to be a kid and go to school and try to get along with her friends. And surely I can do all that while being in a play after school?

"I'm proud of you," Denny's dad says, but he is mostly looking at Denny's mother, whose face is pale and whose eyes keep closing. "I'm sorry. It's great. Of course it's great. It's what you've been working for. It's just hard for me to think about anything else. More schedules and more driving around and—Mom's better at all that. But it's great. It's great."

The more times he says *it's great*, the less I believe him.

"I'm good at keeping track of schedules?" the mom says, her tone out of line with the rest of the conversation, like she is talking to someone else, somewhere else. "And you're mad now, that I'm not good at it anymore?" Her voice sounds gray, broken. I hate it.

"That's not what I said," Denny's father says. "I'm sorry."

"I'm sorry too," I say.

The mom shakes her head like this, too, is wrong. "I don't want you to be sorry," she says.

"Why don't you run upstairs and get some homework done. Sandwiches for dinner, okay?" the father tries, and the mom doesn't say anything to this, but her face is still twisting in anger and something else that I don't have a word for.

"Sure. Yes." There was homework assigned that I think I can manage, and a sandwich sounds delicious. I saw students eating them at school, and they looked fascinating, an incredible mix of bread and meats and sauces. "I really did have an amazing day," I try again. It's the sort of thing I would have told Lady Genevive while changing from my evening gowns to my nightclothes.

She would have smiled, at least, and asked for me to tell her the details. Lady Genevive loves details, and I miss handing them over to her.

Still, it's nice to go upstairs and change into pants made of fleece and a gorgeous green item with a hood and a zipper unlike anything I've ever seen before.

The sandwich is delicious too. Salty and hearty. I eat every last bite.

But I have to do it on my own. Denny's dad talks in a quiet voice to Denny's mom. Sometimes his voice rises, like he's desperate for her to listen, and then it settles again, giving up. Eventually he walks her upstairs, and I hear him say, three times in a row, "You need to get help, sweetheart," but she doesn't say anything to that as far as I can hear, and I don't know quite what it means anyway. I just sit at the kitchen table, which is set for three but is only just me.

I stay at the table for a long time after the sandwich is done. Maybe I'm waiting for Denny's dad to join me, but he doesn't. It gets darker and sleepier, and I have to settle for going over the details of the day in my own head, which isn't the worst thing, after all. It's nice, actually, how they belong only to me.

After a very long while, I head upstairs just as Denny's father is heading down.

"She's fine," he says. Nothing has ever felt less true.

"Maybe you could spend some time with her in the morning, though? Before school? I think that would help."

"Okay," I say, but it's hard to imagine what I would do that might help. It's hard to help when you don't know what's wrong. In all my watching of regular girls, they help with small things—like raking lawns and holding their little sisters. It is only princesses who have to worry about bigger things. A mom who goes to bed early and doesn't talk much and seems to be sad and a certain kind of sick seems bigger than what regular girls are supposed to be in charge of.

"She loves you so much," he says.

"Yes."

"She'll get better, Denny. She did it before. She'll do it again. We just have to stay strong and believe in her."

"Of course."

He sounds a little like I do when I talk about dragons and how I will defeat them, and Sorrowfeld and how I will save it. He sounds like he wants it to be true more than it actually is true.

I try to put the thought aside, though. I don't know the ways of the kingdom of Magnolia Bend. I don't know anything at all.

And in some ways, I don't want to. I want to be a

regular girl without any worries for just a little while longer.

I don't get to spend time with the mother the next morning after all. I oversleep and barely have time for a bowl of their not-porridge before running to the bus. Runa still has saved a seat for me, but she doesn't say much.

And she says even less when we walk by the cast list announcement.

My name is right at the top. Or Denny's name is. *Denny Greene—Dorothy.*

Somehow, my heart soars and shakes at the exact same time. Somehow it is the best and worst moment I've lived of Denny's life so far.

Next to me, Runa simmers.

And then, before I can say a word of apology or explanation or celebration or wonder, she turns around and leaves, silent.

In Sorrowfeld, someone would have said *congratulations*.

The Tale of Dragons True

Denny and Runa, age 11

Actually, dragons aren't born from eggs at all. That was a lie. That was something people in Sorrowfeld thought, but they didn't know the truth.

The truth is that all dragons are just humans who don't get to be humans anymore, after falling into the Lake of Leer.

Dragons are just beings who miss the life they once led.

They're angry at what they had to give up. They want to destroy everything so they won't have to remember.

Dragons are just humans who miss the lives they once lived.

They want to destroy the things that remind them of those lives.

They are cursed to stay dragons forever unless

Chapter 21

Denny Greene

"The princesses of Algrandula and Dovedeerling have requested your presence at a tea today," Lady Genevive says in a newly strained, broken voice.

I've spent the morning alone, which seems unusual for what I've come to understand about being a princess. I am almost always surrounded by people performing an odd mix of telling me what I have to do and asking me what I need.

When Runa and I wrote about princesses, we imagined trays of butter cookies and frothy bubble baths and long afternoon walks with princes under parasols. We didn't think much about what would be demanded of princesses, what they might be responsible for. It's been a while since we've thought much about them at all, our focus having turned so sharply to the dragons. When we decided that dragons used to be humans, we fell in love with them. We wrote down everything about what they used to love and how they felt, being without. We discussed their powers, their violence, their drive to destroy, the caves they might gather in, the width of their wings.

And what they missed. Always, always, we wrote about what dragons missed.

I wish we could have given that sort of focus to the princesses too. I wish we'd thought about them beyond pretty crowns and billowy gowns and high heels. I wish we'd considered what it is, exactly, they're supposed to do, as they wait for the battle to arrive. And how they are meant to shoulder the pressure of saving a kingdom. Or even simply where to look when your only friend's father has been ripped from dinner, lifted into the sky by a terrifying dragon, and you are the one meant to save him, but you totally don't know how.

Lady Genevive's eyes are pink and swollen—she's been crying, but it's clear she doesn't want to talk to me about it.

"Tea?" I ask. "Today? With—everything?"

"*Because* of everything," she says. She speaks with a sigh tucked into the corners of her words. There is a green dress folded over her forearms and a collection of flowers and jewels in a basket hanging from her wrist. In spite of the horror of last night, she's here to adorn me.

"They'll tell me what to do?" A spring of hope shoots into being from my heart. Princesses. Older ones, maybe. Wiser, at least. They'll definitely have more experience than I do.

Obviously they'll know things like who they are and what princesses do all day and how they do it and maybe why I'm here. Meanwhile, I don't even know which of the pieces of clothing that Lady Genevive is holding are underwear.

"I don't know what you shall discuss, Princess Auden." Lady Genevive's voice is tight. Pained. "I am not privy to the conversations of royalty."

"I'm sorry," I say, and I mean it to be for everything, but it is obviously not enough, not even close. Lady Genevive shakes her head and brings the dress closer to me. This is all we'll be talking about today, I guess.

"Princess Junebelle of Algrandula prefers dark colors, and Princess Hannah of Dovedeerling despises pinks and purples. Green seemed a wise choice, but it is up to you, of course."

I hate the way she's talking to me—so cold and snapping, the way Sadie spoke to me at my birthday party, and a billion other times when she clearly wished I was someone different, when she needed me to know

I wasn't picking up on the rules of being a sixth grader fast enough.

"Green is nice," I say, and put on the dress, which is heavy and itchy, but I can't say that now, not with Lady Genevive looking at me the way she is. She buttons the back buttons for me and brushes my hair. I could do it myself, but she's holding the brush so firmly and her mouth is in a straight line that is threatening to become a grimace and it feels like anything I do or say might bother her.

She sprays something that smells incredible on my chest and arms, and powders my face with a shimmery mist. This meeting must be important in a way I can't possibly understand. She paints my lips in light pink and my eyelids in lavender—whatever is happening requires a new level of care, and what she's doing works—every brush against my skin, every spray of roses onto my arms has me feeling more regal, more ready to be who she needs me to be.

It's Runa who would really love this. Her mom doesn't let her wear makeup, but when we go into shops, Runa is always unscrewing the tops of jars of things that smell like flowers or baked goods or sunny patches of earth. I wish I could bottle this all up for her—the colors and smells and even the gentle way that Lady Genevive braids my hair—her hands knowing the patterns without having to think about them at all. Runa said she might like to be a dragon, but it's this she would love—the pampering, the silks and satins, the airy tower rooms and thick carpets. Lady Genevive slides a bejeweled clip into my hair. It's heavy, and pinches a little, but I'm sure it looks the way she needs me to look. And it reminds me of Runa too, the tiny yellow clip she gave me nothing in comparison to this ruby and emerald decoration, but still it feels like I'm doing something for her, something she wanted me to do.

"Can I see how I look?" I ask. I want to peer into a mirror and hope that the person looking back at me will be a princess, will be not-me.

"Let me find a mirror," Lady Genevive says. She looks around the room and in the closet until she happens upon something that makes her brow fold, her chin jut out and back again. "Where did you get this?" she asks. "This is a strange mirror. And not very big. If you'd like to see the rest of you, we'll need to go to another bedroom."

I hold my hand out for the small object she's wrinkling her nose at. When it's placed in my hand, it is light and smooth and familiar. It's not a heavy, intricate, beautiful mirror of this world. It's a brightly colored, fun, simple mirror from my own.

"It's from Magnolia Bend," I say mostly to myself.

"Is that a market in town?" Lady Genevive asks, but I can't answer. I'm shocked to see this tiny bit of home. This bit of me. I don't want to let go of it, but gowns don't have pockets, and I can tell Lady Genevive is getting impatient.

I steal a glance at myself—I am painted and strange-looking, playing the part of princess. I set the mirror down carefully, wondering if Princess Auden has found the mirror from her own world sitting in my garden shed. A thousand questions burst in my head, but I don't have time to worry about any of them.

"They're waiting for you in the tea parlor," Lady Genevive says when she deems me appropriately dressed up. I'm waiting for her to say something familiar and friendly, but it's only this stiff, sad version of her that's here with me today. I let her lead me to the tea party, and hope that somehow maybe one of these princesses will become a friend.

But before we get to the French doors that lead to the parlor, Lady Genevive squeezes my arm. It feels the way a gasp sounds.

"Fix it," she says.

I don't know what she means—my hair? My dress? What do I need to fix?

"Listen to them and fix it," she says again, her voice

pleading now, shaky. "Do whatever they want. My father—just get him back. You have to. Figure it out and get him back."

I'm about to say what I keep saying, which is that I don't know how, I don't know anything at all, really. I'm twelve, I'm twelve, I'm twelve. But Lady Genevive is taut with worry, and it's impossible to be honest with her right now.

"Okay," I say instead. "I'll figure out how to—how to do what I need to do."

I want it to feel more true than it does.

I want to be in a garden shed writing the rules, rather than here in a palace trying to learn them.

But I'm used to wanting things I can't have.

I enter the tea parlor. The other princesses are in green too. There are jewels in their hair. There is pink on their lips. And there are teacups in their hands. It doesn't look like a place where people sit around talking about how to battle dragons, but somehow a lot about Sorrowfeld has surprised me.

I don't know what I expect, exactly—some kind of royal greeting? An elaborate type of curtsy or formalities where we kiss cheeks and ask after one another's kingdoms?

Everything Runa and I didn't write is so clear here. We should have been so much more specific. We decided on the outlines of things, and someone filled them in all wrong, like a coloring book of sunsets and rainbows and ocean views scribbled in with only shades of gray.

I wait for the ritual, but there isn't one. Princess Junebelle of Algrandula straightens her back. She doesn't stand to greet me.

"If you can't protect your kingdom," she says instead of hello, "we will banish the dragons ourselves and dethrone you. You are not a princess if you can't defeat a dragon."

She looks at Princess Hannah of Dovedeerling for agreement, and Princess Hannah nods tightly.

"So, um, you're going to help me figure out how to do it?" I ask, even though she pretty much didn't say that at all and maybe said the exact opposite.

Princess Hannah pours me tea, but doesn't look me in the eye. Princess Junebelle offers me a delicate lemon cookie.

"You're twelve, are you not?" Princess Junebelle asks.

"I just turned twelve."

"Then you shouldn't need help," she says. Princess Junebelle and Princess Hannah appear to be a few years older than me, but they're not grown-ups either, even though they speak like them and cross their legs like them and take tiny sips of tea like them. "You're twelve. You have a duty. And if you're unable to live up to your responsibilities, we'll take them on instead."

Princess Junebelle has a cool, surface way of speaking, so that nothing she says sounds any more important than anything else. *Would you like more tea?* sounds exactly the same as *defeat a dragon or we'll take over your kingdom.*

I take more tea.

I listen for the sound of dragons in the sky.

I adjust the too-tight collar of my too-green dress.

"You've done it before?" I ask. I expect them both to nod, maybe tell the tale of the day they saved their kingdoms from dragons, but instead there's a funny pause.

"Well, no," Princess Hannah says. "Not yet. But we can. Of course. We're princesses." Her voice is quiet, like maybe it doesn't quite believe itself.

"Our kingdoms don't have dragons. We haven't let them invade." Princess Junebelle sweeps in, correcting Princess Hannah, making sure her tone stays prickly, sharp. I remember an entry I wrote once about how dragons are drawn only to Sorrowfeld, because of the beauty of its castle, the power of the witch, the sparkliness of the Lake of Leer. It seemed cool at the time—a kingdom so magical dragons didn't bother with other places. We hardly thought of those other kingdoms, sometimes just mentioning their sad mermaids in their green lakes, wishing they could be in Sorrowfeld.

"I didn't *let* them," I can't stop myself from saying.

"No one *let* them. They're, you know, dragons. Grieving humans. Maybe they were citizens of Sorrowfeld at one time and now they want to destroy it because they miss it so much," I say.

I can almost imagine how Runa and I would have written it. A girl who likes sticking her feet in the moat. A brother with a loud laugh who knows where to find the ripest berries. They like to explore the kingdom, but they go too far and find themselves at the Lake of Leer, and they fall in. They miss the moat, the berries, the being a person. They miss Sorrowfeld so much they can't stand to have it exist at all.

"Excuse me?" Princess Junebelle's face does something new, moves from confusion to fear to a sort of disgust. "Everyone knows those pages of your enchanted text are the work of bad magic. Something the witch put in to unsettle us all. Dragons are dragons. Humans are humans. Are you saying you disagree with your Duke Verden's interpretation of your enchanted text? Are you saying you believe what the witch wrote?" She's spitting every few words, which doesn't seem very princess-like at all, but Runa and I never explicitly wrote anything about princesses not being allowed to spit.

"I— Isn't that— I mean, we decided that—" I try to unscramble my mind and my words, but it's taking too long.

"We?" Princess Junebelle looks astonished at that one tiny word. "You and the witch? You're in it together?"

"No. I'm not in it with a witch. I don't know the witch at all." I take a deep breath to try to calm myself down, but it's hard. I'm supposed to sit here and pretend that Duke Verden's interpretation of a book I wrote is the truth? I'm meant to act like he's the one in charge of everything, even though I'm a princess and a writer of the text and an inventor of this whole world?

I'm so tired of pretending away the truth.

"I suggest you defeat the dragons as soon as you can. Or we will do it," Princess Junebelle says in her hard, spiky voice.

Princess Hannah swallows. I wonder how much she believes that she can defeat a dragon. Maybe, maybe, underneath the way she knows how to wear her hair and hold a teacup, she is uncertain too. Even just a little bit.

"I can do it," I say, and I want to believe it.

Chapter 22

Denny Greene

Lady Genevive escorts me back to my bedroom when tea is over. I curtsied goodbye to the princesses, and anyone watching would have seen us as friends, or at least friendly, but I'm shaken up and blistering with a new feeling. It's fuzzy and tight in my chest, making fists of my hands, curling my toes. There's smoke in the sky again, but I need it to stop, just for a few days, so I can get my bearings. Things have been happening too fast—not just here in Sorrowfeld, but at home too. A year ago, Runa and I went on bike rides to the ice cream shop every weekend and were working on a project where we collaged dragons out of magazine cutouts and fabric scraps. Mom wasn't doing well then, either, but Dad was hiding it from me, mostly, telling me not to worry, shooing me away when she was especially out of it or if unexpectedly mean words started coming out of her.

Then more words came, things I never thought I'd hear my mom, or any moms, say, and Dad couldn't make the words stop and it got too hard to hide them and Runa said she didn't like biking because "everyone watches us, it's weird." And we never quite finished the tail of the dragon collage because Runa joined the student council and the soccer team, and she was busy running laps and hanging up streamers in the cafeteria for every holiday.

Runa grew two inches and got a bra, and I stayed exactly the same.

Except Dad told me about how alcoholism comes back sometimes, even when you think it's gone.

I wrote more and more and more about Sorrowfeld so I wouldn't have to think about any of it.

"Can I change out of this?" I ask Lady Genevive. "Are there, like, sweatpants or something? Something comfy?"

"Sweat?" Lady Genevive looks alarmed. "Comfy?" Her nose wrinkles. I haven't mastered the way they speak here, but even if I had, I'd be too tired right now to perform it. I want Lady Genevive to morph into Runa, who knows how to make the perfect microwave nachos and hot chocolate with two dozen marshmallows. I could ask Lady Genevive for hot chocolate, but it would come in a teacup and would taste too rich, too velvety. I want the kind from the packet. I want it burnt and in a mug the size of my head.

"A robe," I say. "Do you have a robe? Or I mean, do I? Have a robe?"

"Of course, yes," she says, but her voice is a knot and she rummages in the closet loudly before coming out with something silky and beautifully embroidered with a hundred flowers, but not exactly cozy. She hands it to me without looking at me. I put it on anyway, and try to remember everything about it, so I can describe it to Runa.

If I ever see Runa again.

My heart stops in my chest. Everything stops. It's been so busy here, so filled with danger and dresses and the haze of confusion that I haven't considered what it means that I'm here. I haven't wondered yet if I will ever return home or if I'm somehow stuck in this place I made up.

"Um, I have a question," I say to Lady Genevive. I try to say it gently. She's folding my clothes and looking out the window like her father might be dropped back off at any moment. I wish he would be; I wish something simple could happen, something to make this all less terrifying.

"Yes?"

"Do people here, um, you know, in the kingdom, obviously there's magic and dragons and stuff, and I wonder if there's ever, like, people switching places?"

"What are you asking about? Switching places?" Lady Genevive looks right at me finally. Her face is contorted with anger, with exasperation. It's a terrible look—wild, the way Mom looks at me sometimes now when I least expect it. Like I've done something horrible, but I have no idea what the horrible thing is.

Tears well up in my eyes. Why is it that everywhere I go, people look at me like that?

I try a quieter voice, which works with Mom sometimes, although what works best is just shutting myself in my room until she's in some other mood. But this is important. Maybe I'm missing something. Maybe there's a way out of all this.

"I just mean, the kinds of magic you—or we—have here, does it ever include, like, two people switching places?" On one hand, I sound ridiculous. But on the other, this is a place where dragons fly around and pluck lords out of their seats at dinnertime. Surely there's other kinds of magic, too, things Runa and I didn't write or draw but that grew in this place anyway.

"I don't know what that means," Lady Genevive says. She throws the clothes she was folding on the ground. Whatever she was keeping stitched up unravels, and I see now that I'm not her friend anymore. "I don't know what you are dreaming up, but you should be focused on only the one task. Defeating the dragons. It's all you have to do, Princess Auden. We will make your meals. We will dress you and keep your schedule and dust every shelf in this palace. All so that you can do your one single job. The job of being a princess."

"I'm trying to—"

"You can't switch places with someone because things are hard. You have to just do the hard thing. You're twelve. It's *time*."

It is one of the only things that Sorrowfeld has in common with my life in Magnolia Bend—the relentlessness of people trying to tell me that twelve is old enough to do things I can't possibly do, people thinking I am a grown-up when I am so clearly a kid. My face flushes with the things I can't say.

"Right," I say instead, just like I say at home when Dad asks me to check on Mom when she hasn't come out of bed in the morning, or that one time when he called me into their room. Mom was red-eyed and looking ill, like she'd eaten something bad. Like she'd eaten something bad every day for the last week. Dad had a hand on her back.

"I'm trying," Mom said. She was crying. She heaved. "I'm trying, you don't believe me, but I'm trying."

"I know you're trying," Dad repeated, and he sounded so tired. "You need— We need to get rid of this, okay? And have some water. It's okay. It's okay." He was holding a bottle of something.

It was not okay.

"No, don't leave, stay here," Mom said, and I know she was still my mom, but she seemed like a little kid, except slurry and sloppy and strange.

"Okay," Dad said. He had a habit of always agreeing with Mom, and it was starting to make less sense for him to do that. "I'll stay here, and Denny can—" He paused like he wasn't sure about what he was going to say next, but then Mom groaned and tears were falling from her eyes and everything about her was urgent and everything about me was quiet and I know how that turns out. "I'm sorry, sweetheart," he said, and he did look sorry. "I need you to take this downstairs, okay? Leave it by the sink. We'll go get some ice cream later, okay? I'm sorry. I'm sorry."

He handed me the bottle of something clear and sharp-smelling. It smelled the way Mom's thermos had smelled lately, like something gone wrong. It smelled like Mom—scary. Once I saw that bottle, I saw ones just like it other places too, sometimes.

Under the sink in the guest bathroom. Behind a long curtain in the living room. Tucked behind books on the shelf.

"Pour it out," he'd said, and it felt wrong, like not the sort of thing a kid was supposed to do, and Mom made a noise like she knew that too, or maybe the noise was just that she didn't want me to pour it out. I felt as sick as she looked, but I did what I was told to do, my knees shaking, the mean, clear liquid swooshing in the sink before spiraling down the drain.

Dad slept on the floor of my bedroom that night, like he knew he'd crossed a line and wanted to make sure I was okay after. I don't know what he really solved, snoring on the floorboards, but he apologized so much I didn't have a chance to yell at him, tell him how not okay that felt. Sometimes Dad's apologies crowded out all the other things that needed to be said.

Not much changed after that, anyway. He forgot about the ice cream. Another bottle appeared. Dad offered to sleep on my floor again, but it seemed silly to say yes, so I said no, I was fine, I was fine, I was fine, and someday Mom would be too.

Lady Genevive doesn't know about any of this, of course. Maybe there isn't even alcohol in Sorrowfeld. I didn't write it in, that's for sure. She only wants me to worry about her father. She won't understand the meaning of the bottle, the sink, the ice cream I never got to eat, the kid I never quite get to be.

There was no one else to help Dad with the bottles, and there is no one else to help Sorrowfeld with the dragons. I swallow, shake my head to clear it of all the memories, and try again to be a princess. I think of Runa, how she wanted me to try to be a girl who was friends with Sadie and Emily. I do it for her, as much as I do it for Lady Genevive, Duke Verden, Sorrowfeld.

I don't know how to fix anything at home, but here in Sorrowfeld, I know where to look. Maybe here, I can do what's expected of me.

I take down *The Tale of Dragons True* from the shelf. I don't want to talk to Lady Genevive anymore. I don't want advice from princesses from other kingdoms. I want to talk to Runa. To myself.

Reading it again is strange, like reading my own brain, like remembering dreams I had years ago, when I was the same person but totally different.

Only a true princess can defeat a dragon, Runa and I wrote once, so long ago I don't even remember it. *She knows in her heart how to do it. No one else can help her.*

It's exactly the sort of thing we were always writing when I didn't know that the words we were writing would become true. If I'd known, I would have written other rules, about everyone who could help a princess, and what exactly the princesses did for the defeating.

I turn pages and pages, remembering and forgetting and remembering again when we wrote these words, why we wrote them, what we thought they meant.

The Tale of Dragons True is a lot of half pages and elaborate drawings, and stories that don't lead anywhere and never really finish. But still, I remember Runa next to me, laughing at what I came up with, furiously scribbling details that she didn't want to forget. I remember who we were, writing this.

Maybe in Magnolia Bend, Princess Auden is wondering why there's no book that is the history of what it is to start middle school, to live with a mother who is not doing very well. There is no book of rules for how to be popular or when you'll get your period or what it means, even, if you don't have a crush on any sort of person at all, you only really have a crush on long afternoons in the garden shed and the way it feels to sing all the parts in *The Sound of Music* on a rainy day when no one is listening.

That book doesn't exist.

This one does. And it's mine. Those princesses judging me, they don't know Sorrowfeld like I do. I'm so tired of everyone telling me I have to solve everything, then hating the suggestions I have to solve it.

My dad doesn't know what to do, and neither does Princess Junebelle or Duke Verden or even Lady Genevive. They're asking me to figure it out. And maybe, maybe I actually can. I grip the book hard. My book.

"You're not really supposed to spend this much time with the text without my father here to help—" Lady Genevive begins, and this is it, this is the last thing I can listen to, this is the last time I can be told what is real and what isn't by someone who doesn't know, who refuses to see.

"I don't need someone to help me read this!" I explode at her. "This is my kingdom! I don't know every single thing about how to defeat dragons, but I know Sorrowfeld. I know what's real."

When I say it, it becomes true.

No, that's not right—it has always been true. When I say it, I remember that it's true.

It doesn't matter if Duke Verden says the dragons are just dragons. I *know* they are humans. I know about the witch. The Lake of Leer. The wishing for a past you can't have. I know it all. It belongs to me.

I believe in the things Runa and I wrote. I read the first entry we wrote about dragons being humans.

They are cursed to stay dragons forever unless

"Is there another copy of the book?" I ask Lady

Genevive. "It looks like this page got erased or something? Maybe, like, a printer error?"

"There are other copies," she says, "but they're all the same. You know the book has missing moments. Sometimes they get filled in. Sometimes they don't." Her words bite, her frustration with me growing and growing.

"So sometimes it just doesn't tell you everything?" I ask. "That's part of the enchantment?"

"All this time have you just been paying zero attention? My father spent all his time helping you, and now here you are, when he needs you, and you don't even remember a thing about it!"

Lady Genevive sits on the ground and covers her face with her hands. I'm mad at her, I feel bad for her, I understand her, I wish she was Runa. I'm buzzing with contradictions and heartaches and certainties.

I hang on to the book. The book is what's real. The book is what I can count on. *Stop asking other people for answers to questions you already have the answers for,* I tell myself.

I flip through more pages. Some are detailed and extensive, others have these half sentences, these unwritten words, these missing moments. I read the pages, one after the other after the other, and realize what should have been so obvious all along. It's not part of an enchantment. *The Tale of Dragon True*'s missing moments are the moments that Runa and I ran off to do something else—eat cereal or play Nintendo or do homework or get in a fight about whether the better part in *Wicked* is Elphaba or Glinda. Some days we had all the time in the world, some days we got bored easily and moved on. And recently, many days, we started to write and then stopped because Runa wanted to go to someone's birthday party or try on new bathing suits or make a list of the people in class who we liked the most, and the people in class who we thought liked us the most, and the people in class we wanted to like us more.

Those lists are in other notebooks, in corners of our bedrooms or stuffed into backpacks.

Except for one. I flip to the back of *The Tale of Dragons True* and see what Runa wrote only a few days ago, or maybe a hundred years, depending on how time works in Sorrowfeld. It is the list of ideas for our birthday party, the new ones that I hated, the ones we tried but that didn't work, the compromises that failed to be enough of what Runa needed them to be.

"What about this?" I ask, showing it to Lady Genevive.

"A message from the witch," Lady Genevive says, proud to know the answer. "My father hasn't deciphered it fully yet, but it's very important. Dangerous."

Chocolate frosting, the list says. *Twister. Elegant decorations. Some purple. No costumes. Cool music.*

"Huh," I say.

I don't want to call Lady Genevive's missing father a liar. But the things he's been telling her aren't true.

The Tale of Dragons True

Denny and Runa, age 7

In Sorrowfeld you have to tell the truth.

If not, you will be punished.

Maybe by dragons or witches. Or maybe by princesses. Princesses are powerful too. They aren't just fancy.

But they are really fancy.

Chapter 23

Princess Auden

Mr. Lowen, the theater teacher, opens the first day of rehearsals by showing us all someone else playing Dorothy. The woman doing it is so pretty, and her face fills up a whole screen hanging in the auditorium. She looks sad and shaky, and I've never heard anyone sing like her, including me.

"*The Wizard of Oz,*" Mr. Lowen says in a scratchy voice that reminds me so much of Duke Verden I nearly topple out of my chair, "is a story about a lost girl, far away from home, who is scared and needs others to help her find her way. We'll be using Judy Garland's performance as inspiration for our show."

Everyone in the room nods. Mr. Lowen says it like it's right for us to borrow from someone else's idea of this story, but I thought at least here, in this one tiny space, I'd get to figure something out for myself.

"Yes, there in the cat ears?" Mr. Lowen says. He doesn't ask the name of the girl whose hand is raised, and he doesn't look at her when she speaks.

"This movie is, like, really old? And maybe we want to bring in some more modern stuff, newer ideas about, like, the story and what it means to us?" The girl's voice is clear and strong. She still seems familiar in a way that makes me feel warm and shiny. She would make an incredible princess—so sure and solid, able to take charge of a situation with ease.

Mr. Lowen shakes his head swiftly. "What it means to *you*?" he scoffs. "Don't worry about what it means to you. I'm the director, and this is an homage to Judy Garland, a celebration of one of the greatest performances of all time—this is a time capsule."

No, I suppose the girl in the cat ears is not a princess after all. No one here is a princess, I realize. Mr. Lowen throws instructions at us, tells us how to say lines, what to think about while we're saying them, where to stand, and even how to feel about what we are doing.

"You should be disappointed in yourselves," he says when there is too much giggling and forgetting of the way we're supposed to move around the stage, "for not working hard enough on this. For not focusing on this moment here, our journey together. The theater is serious business, and you've been given an opportunity to be in that seriousness."

Sadie nods, yes yes yes, and I can see Mr. Lowen watching her agreement. I don't nod, because I don't agree. Dragons are serious business. Ruling a kingdom. Whatever is happening with Denny's mom, that is certainly serious business. But theater is pretend. Theater is singing words that other people wrote and wearing someone else's clothes and telling a story that maybe someone will relate to some tiny part of, and it's making that story feel alive, which is exciting, yes, but it isn't serious, not the way so many other things are serious.

The way Runa is looking at me is serious—like she's supposed to do something but she doesn't know what and maybe never will.

I do the lines the way it feels good to do them, and Mr. Lowen grumps around but doesn't correct every single one, even though I can tell he wants to. I sing notes that feel impossible, at first, to reach, and then somehow come out, surprising even me. That's my favorite part of singing. How it surprises my own ears, how I have to trust my voice to do something I'm telling it to do, but I won't really know until I've done it if I'm able to.

All week I watch Mr. Lowen scowl at most of what

I'm doing and scribble notes into a black leather notebook with straight lines and small, tight handwriting on every page. It is not a notebook that matches *The Wizard of Oz*, which is full of golden bricks and shining shoes and nothing so heavy or straightforward as that notebook.

Still, the best part of every day is rehearsal, where I get a break from playing Denny and get to play Dorothy. Dorothy's easier. She has lines and friends and a purpose.

Denny is impossible to play. I keep messing it up. On Tuesday I wear a beautiful shimmery blue gown to school, and I'm informed it's a Halloween costume belonging to someone named Elsa, not clothing, and no one can explain the difference, and Runa whispers to me in the bathroom, "You have to stop doing stuff like this, Denny. I can't keep explaining this stuff to everyone. I don't want to. I want to just be normal."

I try to ask Denny's parents what I should wear, but Denny's mom is hard to speak to after school—she is muddled and sleepy in the afternoons and evenings, and shakes her head at almost everything I say, her eyes sometimes filling with tears, like she'd like to help but can't.

Denny's dad says not to put so much pressure on her. It seems like talking to me about almost anything is pressure, so I stop asking her much at all.

But when I come downstairs Wednesday in jeans and a soft pale green sweater, she gives me a smile that she must have learned long, long ago, before whatever happened to her that made her so sad.

"You look beautiful in that, Denny," she says. "I hope you feel good in it." Her smile is starry and brilliant, big. I would do anything to make it happen again, I'd wear a hundred pale green sweaters, I'd wear nothing else for the rest of my life if it meant she'd smile like that.

This is what it is to have a mother. A real one. It's everything I thought it would be, everything I only vaguely remember it being. I want to grasp it, hold it in my hands.

Save it, so that Denny can have it later, too.

"Thank you," I say.

"Want me to do French braids for you?" she asks. "I know it's been a while, but we have time this morning."

"I'd love that," I say.

She brushes my hair, then pulls and prods it into two perfect French braids. It is a familiar feeling, someone else doing my hair, but it's also a completely unknown feeling. A *mom* doing my hair. She sort of hums to herself while she does it, and she asks if she's pulling too hard. She smooths down bits that don't even need smoothing. At the end she sweeps a finger along my cheek and I smile into that tiny touch.

"I did it," she says, and she sounds so filled with pride, but also a little sad, like she should have been doing it every morning, all along, and I think maybe she will.

But she doesn't.

On Thursday she is still in bed when I come downstairs and when I knock on the door to ask about braids, she rustles in bed but doesn't reply.

I wear the right clothing that day, but in class we're doing a unit on Greek mythology and I ask why they don't think any of the stories are true, because they all sound possible enough to me and I want to know how they determine here what's real and what's not. "Does someone interpret it all and tell you which parts are true?" I ask, thinking maybe I'll figure out who does Duke Verden's work here, and there's a terrible mixture of laughter and silence in response. The teacher tells me not to be rude and asks if I need to stay after class. I tell him I don't need to, but I'm available because no one likes having lunch with me, and he tightens his jaw and tells me to write a page about how Greek mythology is relevant to our world today.

I write one page about how lucky people here are to not have dragons or cyclops, and on Friday, I'm given detention. It sounds like a punishment, but instead it is a glorious hourlong break where I sit in a room and think my own Princess Auden thoughts and don't have to try to translate them into Denny-ness.

I go to rehearsal after detention, feeling wonderful. But I've missed an hour of rehearsal, and Mr. Lowen is even more angry than usual, and Sadie is running my lines and singing my songs while they wait for me. When I replace her onstage, she tightens her whole face.

"You think you're so great," she whispers while she walks away.

"I don't think I'm great at all," I say back, but I don't whisper and everyone hears me. There's that same mix of laughter and silence; Sadie's laughter and silence are both the loudest.

Runa gives me a look like I'm doing this all on purpose, like I've chosen to ruin something that was good, and I don't know how to explain to her that actually this is me doing my best, I'm just that bad at being Denny.

"I don't know what's going on with you," she says at the very end of rehearsal on Friday, "but you obviously have decided you don't want to fit in."

"I do want to," I say. "I don't know how." It's the truth, or as much of it as I can tell her.

Runa looks sad, and I know the look. Duke Verden has given me the look a million times, and I always hate it.

"Try harder," Runa says, which is better than telling me to stop trying, that I've already failed too much to recover. But it feels like a little earthquake to my heart, which is already trying so hard. "I know your mom is sick and stuff, but it can't always be about that. I keep trying to help you, but you don't care! This matters too. Getting along with everyone. Fitting in. This matters to me." Runa takes a deep breath, tenses her jaw, and I can see that even though I don't understand it, it's her truth.

"I've never had to try to fit in before," I say, and that truth is mine.

It coils up with the other truth—Runa doesn't know how to be the friend Denny needs. The friend I need.

Princess Auden

I try, but it isn't enough. Trying is weird here. How hard I try doesn't seem to have anything to do with how I end up. Sometimes, actually, it seems like if I try harder, I somehow end up even worse.

Which is probably why by the end of the third week of rehearsals, Runa is barely speaking to me. Sadie, in the role of the Scarecrow, won't look me in the eye, even onstage, and Emily pretends not to hear me when I try to talk to her. The only person who is really engaging with me is Mr. Lowen, with his thick glasses and big beard and notebook that gets heavier and more full of complaints about me every day.

"Sadder, Denny," he says for the hundredth time.

"She's scared. She's a scared girl in a new world. You need to hunch, maybe. Or cry. She needs to be frightened. You need to be frightened."

According to Mr. Lowen, Dorothy is this scared mouse of a girl. He wants her to tiptoe into rooms. He wants her to shiver every time she meets one of her new friends. He wants her to let the Scarecrow and the Tin Man lead the way down the Yellow Brick Road, while she follows nervously behind.

"What am I supposed to be scared of?" I ask. I'm polite. I'm a princess; I am always polite. But I've asked some version of this question so many times that I suppose it no longer feels polite to Mr. Lowen or anyone else watching. Sadie rolls her eyes. A boy named George who is playing the Tin Man slumps over, like it's going to be too long an interlude to even stay upright for.

"The world," Mr. Lowen says. "She's in a new world. We've been over this, Denny. Imagine yourself in a whole new place, with whole new rules. Imagine that everything you know and love is gone, and you're being expected to figure out a new way to be. Try to imagine that. You would be scared. You'd barely be able to function. I want to see that coming through your performance." Mr. Lowen sighs after practically every word.

"I *am* imagining that," I say, which is a sort of lie.

I'm not imagining it, exactly; I'm living it. And it does not feel the way Mr. Lowen says it should. "I'm imagining that, and I think Dorothy would feel excited and courageous and maybe proud of herself for all she's doing. I think she might be excited that she's become so beloved here in Oz so quickly. And excited she's made friends."

My voice clenches around the word *friends*, because it is the place my life and Dorothy's seem to diverge. Dorothy travels to Oz and makes beautiful new friends who help her figure herself and her goals out. And they help get her home.

I came to Magnolia Bend and lost all the friends Denny had. In Sorrowfeld, everyone admires a princess. But the thing I've been scared of is turning out to be true: that no matter how often I watched them from my tower, I don't know anything about being a normal girl.

"If you don't think you're up to this," Mr. Lowen says, "we have someone else able to be Dorothy. A play is a group activity. It's a collaboration. And we need collaborative performers. If you don't feel you can be that, Denny, then I know someone else would be happy to take over."

I'm not sure Mr. Lowen would actually do that this late in the game, but Sadie's eyes light up at the very thought of it. And for a moment, it almost seems like a valid choice. Maybe it's what I should do. If I give up and Sadie gets to be Dorothy, then maybe they'll all forgive me and I'll have friends and then I'll finally be like one of those girls playing across the moat with bare feet and big smiles.

But Denny wanted this part. That's something I know for sure, from sheets of practice music and the novel version of *The Wizard of Oz* in her bedroom, all marked up with underlines and highlights and notes in the margins about how different moments might inform her performance. I can't lose something else of hers.

"I'm up to it," I say, and I try again to sing the way he wants me to, which feels wrong and boring and lost.

There's a bustle at the end of rehearsal. It's always this way—everyone is loud and clumsy, packing backpacks, trying dance moves, diving into their phones, whispering secrets, shouting songs. In the middle of it, Runa comes up to me.

"You don't even seem very happy," she says. I'm trying to remember when she last spoke to me. Maybe last week, when she asked what I was eating for lunch? I sit at her table at lunch most days, unless she seems especially irritated by me, but I don't talk, and no one talks to me. And I sit near her on the bus, but she and Sadie and Emily are always huddled together, their heads touching, their voices too soft for me to even know what it is I'm being left out of.

I hadn't thought Runa was paying any attention to me. But she noticed something real about me.

Lady Genevive would never be comfortable enough to make such an observation. And I would never reply the way I reply now.

"I'm not happy," I say.

The words release something in me. I tried to do the French braids Denny's mom did in my hair, but they came out all wrong—chunks of hair not making their way in, bumps everywhere, an uneven pattern. It almost feels like I made it up. So I have messy French braids and Mr. Lowen telling me all the ways I am playing my part wrong, even though my part is me, and Sorrowfeld is unreachable and maybe destroyed by now, and I am stuck here, in a world that doesn't make any sense, a place I can't possibly fit into, even though I thought I would fit into a place where I didn't have to be a princess.

I'm not much of a princess, and I'm not much of a real girl, and according to Mr. Lowen, I'm not much of a Dorothy either, so no. I'm not happy. I'm not happy and I don't know how to be happy. I am wrong everywhere

I go. I'm a disappointing princess and a disappointing Denny.

But Runa—she's not perfect either. The girls playing in the moat seemed so much happier in their friendship than Runa and Denny seem to be. If one of those girls fell in the water, the others picked her up. If one was sad, the others made her laugh.

"I'm not happy," I say again, a thing I wouldn't dare say in Sorrowfeld, but surely here, as a normal girl, I can say one single true thing?

I take a step closer to Runa, who looks like she might hug me, might make it better in some tiny or big way.

But Runa doesn't hug me.

"You don't want to step down?" she says instead. "Maybe Dorothy is too much pressure?"

She isn't here to comfort me. She's here to give my part to Sadie. It's hard to breathe. All that matters to Runa is Sadie.

"Singing 'Over the Rainbow' is the only part of the day that *does* make me happy," I say, staying honest.

"Don't be dramatic," Runa says, and my heart breaks. For me and also for Denny, who thinks this is her best friend, who deserves so much better.

If I ever meet Denny, I want to ask her what it was that made her and Runa friends. What they liked about each other. What they talked about. Maybe if

I had more information, I'd know how to get us back there.

"Being Denny is hard," I say, which I can tell sounds weird to Runa, who thinks I *am* Denny. "I mean, things are hard for me right now."

She softens a little. "I know. And that's really big. And you think everything that matters to me is kinda small."

I nod. She's sort of right. There are dragons. There are sick moms. It's hard to care about much else. But I can try. For Denny, who is maybe saving my kingdom. I can try to find a way to care about what Runa cares about.

"Look, I'm having a sleepover tonight," Runa says, a little unsure of the words coming out.

"Okay." It isn't an invitation, it's just some sort of alert, so I'm not sure how to respond.

"I still want you there. I do. You're— We're— I still want to do this all with you."

I want to ask what *this all* means. Growing up, I guess. Becoming popular. Being twelve.

She goes on before I can clarify. "But don't do any baby stuff. Don't talk about dragons. Or Sorrowfeld. Don't mention Sorrowfeld."

The whole world stops for an instant. I'm sure I must have misheard Runa. The name of my kingdom coming out of her mouth is all wrong.

"Sorrowfeld?" My hands fly to my heart like it might leave my chest and it's my job to keep it locked in my ribs.

"Yeah, don't talk about it. Like, at all. Honestly, we should throw away *The Tale of Dragons True*. Or burn it. If anyone ever saw it— I mean, seriously, Denny. Can you do something with it?"

"*The Tale of Dragons True* is here?" My heart is beating so fast I'm getting dizzy. I stiffen my legs so I don't fall over, and I reach out for the wall to stabilize me.

"*Here?* You brought it to school?"

"What? No, I didn't bring anything to school. I just meant— I didn't know you had— I don't know where it is. The, um, thing you're talking about." My brain is rushing to try to make sense of Runa suddenly talking about my home like it's a part of her home, like it's a thing she knows about. But it feels like a jigsaw puzzle with all the wrong pieces.

"Okay. Well, don't bring it to my house either."

"Your house?"

"The sleepover!" Runa says. She rolls her eyes. Sighs. "The sleepover that really matters to me, even though it's not as big a deal as all your stuff!"

It's hard to think about anything else. That Runa, of all people, knows about *The Tale of Dragons True*. That maybe it's somewhere at Denny's home.

"Right, sleepover," I say, but I'm hot with overwhelm and itching to go back to Denny's home, to see my book, to add to the puzzle I've been trying to solve since I landed here.

Runa glances at me, cringes a little at the way I look. "Wear your hair down. And you need cute pajamas. You can borrow my polka-dot ones. Don't talk about the play. Don't sing. And seriously, no dragons. We don't do dragons anymore. Sorrowfeld is over. Okay?"

My warmth toward her that I'm trying to build on shrinks. She wants me to care about the things she cares about, but she wants me to show that by taking orders. Making myself small. Making myself into nothing.

Sorrowfeld is not over. Dragons fly through the skies in the place her actual best friend is. And she hasn't even noticed that I am not the real Denny. That I am a princess. And princesses don't take orders and don't wear their hair down and don't get told what to talk about. And princesses especially don't give up on their kingdoms.

"I'm not going to keep apologizing for not being exactly who you think I should be, Runa. And I don't think I'm the only one who's been messing up," I say.

She looks shocked at the words, her lips pursing,

opening to say something, closing again as her brow furrows.

I don't care what she says. I'm the last remaining princess of Sorrowfeld, the one who will defeat the dragons.

Sorrowfeld is not over, and neither am I.

Chapter 25

Princess Auden

Denny's parents are fighting in the kitchen when I get home.

Denny's father sees me and puts a hand on Denny's mom, maybe to make them pause the fight, but it backfires, and she shoves his hand from her shoulder.

"You think you know everything, you think you're so perfect and can sit around judging me. You just sit around judging me all day, how is anyone supposed to live like that, with someone breathing down their neck, you think you just know all of everything all the time!" Denny's mom is shouting, and her voice is unfamiliar, the words winding and strange, repeating themselves, folding back onto each other. My heart thumps. I didn't know the way someone's voice sounded could be scary. I didn't know the repeating of words and phrases could feel so bad. I touch my own hand, as if mine is the one she shoved.

Denny's dad just mumbles in return, "Okay, all right, okay, calm down, take a breath," and this only seems to make Denny's mom angrier and more confused-sounding.

"You calm down! You! You're sooooo calm, right? So calm down, right?"

"I don't know," Denny's dad says, the words broken, bruised. That's scary too. He doesn't sound like a grown-up anymore. And we need a grown-up here.

Denny's mother turns toward me at last.

"You used to be on my side," she says, anger and hurt and dizziness all baked into the words. I feel myself shrink. And before I can ask what that means or why she looks woozy or what it is she's so mad about anyway, she storms out of the kitchen and out of the house.

"She just needs to cool down," Denny's dad says in a voice that shudders. "She does that sometimes. Sits on the porch and gets herself together."

I just stare.

"She's gotten better before," he says. "She'll do it again." It sounds like a chant, a thing he says a million times a day, to himself, to her, and now to me.

"Okay," I say.

But it isn't. The small, shrunken feeling doesn't stop. It's a new one for me, but I get the sense that it isn't a new feeling for Denny. I hope in Sorrowfeld she gets to feel big and powerful. I hope in Sorrowfeld she knows how strong she is to have survived this kingdom here.

Sorrowfeld. I gather myself up.

"Um, Dad? Do you know anything about a dragon book?" I ask, trying to stay focused on what I came here to do.

"*The Tale of Dragons True?* Sure," he says.

In the quickness and rightness of that answer, I know that there has been a time that he has known Denny well, that he has paid attention to the words she's said, that he has kept track of things like her favorite colors and her math homework and the title of the book of dragon lore she has with her best friend. I wish I could know that version of Denny's father. He'll probably meet the French-braiding version of Denny's mother somewhere.

"Where's the book?" I ask, before he turns his attention again to his work or the work of worrying about Denny's mother.

"I assume in the shed, why? Is it not there?"

"The shed out back?"

"Of course." For one crystallized moment, Denny's father looks at me like he might have the time to try to figure me out.

But I'm not going to give it to him. I head out to the backyard, to the tiny shed I'd imagined at first was a dragon's lair but I now know to be something many people in this kingdom have—a little storage space in their backyards for watering cans and lawn mowers and bikes. Or, in the case of Denny, apparently, dragons.

I've gotten used to Denny's dragon dolls and figurines in her room, but there are even more out here. There are drawings and paintings and sculptures and writings. There are pillows and blankets on the ground, mostly in dragon patterns. There is a dragon lamp. A dragon pencil.

And something I hadn't seen when I first arrived. Something that stops my breath for a moment before it can begin again. It's a dragon mirror. It is a heavy metal object that could fit in the castle, and the look of it—finally familiar after so much that has been strange and new—chokes me up a little.

It is an item that belongs in Sorrowfeld. I've seen it before, somewhere in the castle that I can't quite recall. And wow, I miss Sorrowfeld so much it is hard to stand, hard to breathe.

So I sit on the ground, and the book is right there in

front of me, as casually dropped as shoes by the front door, a sweater on the back of a chair, a glass of water abandoned halfway through. It doesn't look familiar—it's a leather notebook, but nothing like Mr. Lowen's. This one is beaten up by weather and time and worry and wonder.

When I open it, what's inside is scribbled in too-light pencil and too-bright neon-pink marker and too-messy blue pen. It is an object entirely from this world. No royal cursive or embossing or heft. The words inside are written in slopes and slants, sentences crashing from one corner of the page to the next, letters collapsing against one another or so far apart they almost don't look like they're in the same word. Some sections written so fast and tiny they're hard to read, others written out with precision and bullet points and accompanying illustrations.

We don't have any documents in Sorrowfeld that look anything like this. Maybe it's just a strange overlapping coincidence.

But then I start to read.

And the words—not the look of them, not at all, but the actual things they're saying—are practically baked into me. Rules of dragons. Histories of dragons. Maps of where dragons are thought to live.

This is our book. My book. *The Tale of Dragons True.*

Here in Magnolia Bend, it looks chaotic and messy and childish, but everything else about it is our official book on confronting the dragons of Sorrowfeld.

My brain tries to make sense of it. Everything I've ever been told to be true, everyone I've tried to be, every rule I've tried to follow—it's all in this book.

All this time we were told it was an enchanted text, a magical thing that we needed Duke Verden's careful help interpreting. But really the only person who understood any of it was Denny.

And Runa.

My whole world, just the imagining of a couple of best friends, normal girls who thought it would be fun to imagine a not-at-all normal life.

I flip through it again and again, trying to tie the markers-and-mayhem look of it to the sturdy, regal version I know and coming up more and more confused with every page turn. The way it's written and drawn here—in silver sparkly marker, with misspellings and clumsy letters and forgotten sentences—feels so entirely unserious. A bit of fun.

But somewhere else, this is all real. Dragons in the sky. Kingdoms under threat. Princesses turning twelve, taking on royal responsibilities.

I flip through again, looking for answers. Maybe there's something in here about a princess who finds herself far away from her kingdom, and what it is she's supposed to do about it. But I don't see anything.

It feels so irresponsible, what they've done. They wrote these rules and stories and little bits of history and then they drew pictures that turned real and they scribbled out old rules and wrote new ones, and all along, they were the witches, they were the ones in charge.

Kids. Little kids in the strangest kingdom on earth, telling me who I had to be.

I can't make it make sense.

And there's no time to make it make sense.

Denny's father is calling to me from the front yard.

"She didn't go outside to cool down, she went in the car," he says, scared and shaking. "I went outside to try to talk to her again, and it's gone, the car, and she's gone, and she went in the car, she went in the car, we have to do something."

I hate the word *we*. I am not a princess here, but still, somehow, I'm supposed to be making grown-up decisions, having grown-up conversations.

"She went in the car where?" I ask.

"It's doesn't matter, Denny," he says. "She's been drinking. She can't drive. She can't drive." He's rushing to the garage to look at the place where the car isn't, and I'm trying to make sense of his words, which are new but also feel right, feel like a truth I knew all along. I don't know what it means, to drink, or what she's been drinking. But I've seen bottles of drinks in odd places—a coat closet, the cabinet that otherwise only has mixing bowls, Denny's parents' bedroom.

Denny's father is discussing out loud all the possibilities—trying to follow her in the car, calling the police, running after her, waiting at home and hoping she comes back soon—when we hear the sirens. And I think I know before he does. Maybe because I know what it feels like—the moment before everything changes.

We hop in the other car and drive to where the sirens are, which is also where Denny's mother is. It takes only a minute to get there, but somehow in that minute that she drove, everything changed.

We get out of our car and look at hers.

It's smashed against a tree, dented, battered, broken. Denny's mother is bruised and crying and slumping but alive, which is all Denny's father can say over and over again. "Oh, thank god she's alive, she's alive, she's alive."

And she is. She's alive.

Within a few minutes, she's being carried into an ambulance called by a construction worker who watched it happen. A police officer is talking to Denny's dad and then to me, but I don't know what he says or what I say. And then she's being taken away, not by dragons, but by something else, something maybe even harder to understand.

In Sorrowfeld, there are just dragons. Dragons and witches, and we know how to fear those things and what they can do to us. But here there are things to fear that I didn't know about. Cars and moms and drinks and excuses and turns in the road and misunderstandings and so many other things, too many to list.

I hate how much there is to be afraid of here, and how much there is to try to understand.

Denny's father grips my shoulders and says in this awful, small voice, "We should have done more, we should have tried harder."

Maybe the real Denny would have known how to get her mother out of bed, how to have her eat sandwiches and sip lemonade instead of filling up that one blue thermos that she always seemed to be carrying around. Maybe the real Denny has that kind of magic.

But I don't think so. I don't think anyone does.

These adults are asking us to defeat dragons and save mothers and then they're mad when we don't do it, but *they* don't know how to do it either. An anger stirs up in my stomach, moves to my throat.

I don't have an enchanted text here, but some rules don't have to be written down.

We *should not have done more*, I think to myself. *You. Her. Not we. I am a kid. How would I know how to fix this?*

We watch the ambulance drive away with Denny's mom inside. We watch the construction worker shake his head at the mess of the car, at the mess of us.

I'd thought coming to Magnolia Bend was a chance to feel like one of those kids without all the responsibilities and promise and pressure. I want to go to rehearsal and sing and—oh! I almost forgot about tonight!—sleep over at Runa's and say the right things and watch movies and not care about anything at all except that exact, midnight moment when we would all hush into whispers before falling asleep.

I want that. I want to call Runa and tell her what happened, but the thought vanishes because there's sirens and lights and this feeling in my chest like things are all changing forever. And instead of giving Runa another thought, I get into the car with Denny's dad, and we follow the ambulance to the hospital, where we wait and wait and wait to hear what we already know.

That Denny's mom has a problem with drinking.

That Denny's mom is in trouble.

That something has to be done about Denny's mom.

The Tale of Dragons True

Runa, age 10

Once upon a time, there lived a witch in a terrifying castle. She lived upon the Lake of Leer, and she was a terrible witch, she wished nothing but harm upon the great kingdom of Sorrowfeld.

Maybe the witch used to be a different kind of witch, the good kind with love spells and fairy dust, but she became cruel over time, having been an outsider in the kingdom for too long.

The witch played a terrible game with the people of Sorrowfeld. She named it the Witch's Wander. The people of Sorrowfeld thought they could win this game the witch invented. But a witch never invents a game she can lose.

Really, the witch always wins.

Chapter 26

Princess Auden

The next morning, Runa, Emily, and Sadie are at my door. It's past ten but I'm still in pajamas and haven't had breakfast yet. The sun hurts my eyes. "Hey," I say. "You guys want to, um, come inside or something? Oh! Or we can go out to the shed. Right, Runa?" I'm proud of myself for remembering that that seems to be where so much of their friendship happens. It feels like the right thing to offer.

But it isn't. Of course it isn't.

"You're not even going to say you're sorry?" Runa asks, and her voice sounds raw, hurt. But I'm too tired to know what I'm supposed to be apologizing for. I rub my eyes and wish for the millionth time that Denny had left me a list of rules for this impossible world of hers.

"Never mind," Runa says, seeming to gather herself up. "I came over to tell you we can't be friends anymore." She looks over at Sadie for some sort of validation that this is the correct thing to say, that she is delivering the message they have clearly discussed.

I know a formal message when I see one. Kings and dukes and other princesses visit Sorrowfeld often to tell me all manner of things—that we need to come up with new laws for the witch by the Lake of Leer to obey, that certain magic potions need to be better sanctioned. That the border between our kingdoms is drawn wrong. That they are furious about some infraction from Duke Verden. That our trees are too tall. That more dragons are coming.

Runa looks like she's about to tell me more dragons are coming.

I'm so bleary from the night in the hospital and then back home, trying to sleep. I can't make sense of her words. "We can't be friends?"

"You can't just not show up. I went out of my way to invite you, I'm trying so hard to make this work with you, and you don't even care enough to tell me you're not coming."

"She was so upset last night," Sadie says, looking a little too happy about it. "*So* upset."

Runa nods and continues. "On top of everything

happening with *Wizard of Oz* and how weird you've been lately—we just can't be friends with someone so mean."

Something in her face flutters with these words, like she doesn't entirely believe them but feels she has to say them. I know that feeling too—speeches I don't want to give filled with words I'm not sure I believe. But it doesn't help the hurt, and the flutter unflutters itself quickly. She turns her face steely and sure.

"Oh."

I don't know what to say or if this is generally how things work in Magnolia Bend.

I am not one of the girls across the moat. Wherever I go, there are dragons.

"Friends don't act this way," Sadie says. She looks pleased to deliver this news, and she holds Runa's hand for some kind of support.

"You don't understand, last night got really complicated and I had to stay here and it's hard to explain, but it wasn't because I didn't want to come." I am speaking quickly, trying to fix the broken thing between us. But I know even as I'm saying the words that they're not going to give me a chance to explain and that I've said it wrong, too. Runa seems to know that something is wrong with Denny's mother, but the other girls might not, and I'm not sure if anyone outside of me and Denny's parents knows just how bad it is.

"We don't need explanations," Sadie says. I look at Runa to try to understand if she agrees. "We tried to include you, but you obviously don't want to be one of us."

I sigh. It's exhausting. Being Denny. Explaining myself. Being told I'm terrible when I'm just trying to get through each day. "Well, I suppose, yes, that's true. I would just like to be me."

"Exactly." Sadie rolls her eyes, and Emily rolls hers too, and Runa looks at the ground. Flutter. Unflutter. Flutter. Unflutter.

Once again, she stays on unflutter. She decides to let this be how it is.

And I guess this is how it is.

I can't fix what's broken here with Runa, but maybe Denny will fix Sorrowfeld. Maybe I can still help with that, somehow. I'm desperate for a sliver of hope.

"Runa, can I just ask you something?" I ask.

"She's not in the mood," Sadie says.

"I'm asking *Runa*," I snap. I think the rules of being Denny would say to be quiet here. But she's off fighting dragons, and I'm tired of trying to be her. My poor imitation of Denny is only making things worse. So I try being Princess Auden instead. "I'm asking my friend whatever I want to ask her. I don't need permission from you." It feels good to hear my own voice, my own words.

"She's not your friend anymore," Sadie says. She grabs Runa's hand like she's hers now, and I wonder what makes her hold on so tightly and need so much. She squeezes Runa's hand, and Runa doesn't know where to look.

"The book," I say to Runa, trying to make her look at me. "*The Tale of Dragons True*. Did we just make it all up? How did we know all that, about Sorrowfeld?"

I know she told me not to talk about the book in front of these girls, but Emily is already stepping away and Sadie is tugging on Runa's shirt and they're all headed somewhere together, I guess—a bike ride around the neighborhood or back to Runa's to watch television and eat pancakes or who knows what else, something I'll never know about or understand, something particular to this impossible kingdom. I need her to tell me *something*, anything, about why the one heavy, complicated, ever-changing book about dragons and kingdoms that I grew up studying is here, in a messy, strange form, in Denny's garden shed.

"Dragons?" Sadie asks. She starts to laugh, letting go of Runa's shirt to focus on the ridiculousness of me.

Runa's jaw clenches. Her eyes narrow into anger.

Not at Sadie and Emily and the way they're trying to control everything. But at me.

"Shut up, Denny," Runa says. "Leave me alone."

With that, she turns away from me and my questions and, I guess, the friendship itself.

I got the role that was supposed to be Sadie's. I missed the party. I brought up the dragons. I didn't wear the right hair clips or the right jeans or the right outfits that match, but not too closely, their outfits. I didn't say the right things about my body or someone else's face.

But I cannot be taken down by Magnolia Bend. I am not going to be this quiet girl letting things happen any longer. I'm not any good at being Denny because I'm not Denny. I can only be me.

Runa and Sadie and Emily walk off to do whatever it is cool girls do in Magnolia Bend on Saturday mornings. A terrible warm feeling rushes my face. I am Princess Auden. The last remaining princess of Sorrowfeld. The one who can save the kingdom.

"Who was that?" Denny's dad asks, ambling down the stairs in his robe and sleepiest expression.

"Runa," I say. "I was supposed to go to her house yesterday."

"Ah, well, family comes first," Denny's dad says. He sounds sorry, sort of, but also certain, and I suppose this is a rule of this kingdom.

But it feels like a particularly hard one to follow. The things Denny's family needs seem enormous and infinite. Dragons are scary, yes, but they are singular. They fly through the kingdom, and you either defeat them or you do not. But Denny's family is not a dragon. They are here, they aren't going anywhere, and what they need shifts and reshapes and grows every day. If family comes first here, how will anything else ever come next?

I want something of mine, of Denny's, to come first. I can't sit here and just be the girl who can't save her friendships and can't save her mom.

I am Princess Auden, I say to myself again and again until I remember that it's true.

"I have rehearsal today," I say. It's in the afternoon, and it will probably be wildly uncomfortable now that I have no friends, but opening night is looming, and even in the worst circumstances, it still feels good to play the role of Dorothy instead of the role of Denny. Dorothy has friends and ruby slippers and a very specific yellow path to follow.

Plus, I know what happens in the end for Dorothy. I know she finds her way home.

"Oh, Denny, no, not today. We need to visit Mom in the hospital. She needs to see you. Maybe with everything happening, it makes sense to have your understudy take over." Denny's dad looks at the ground. "There will be other plays. Right now—what happened yesterday—it's too much. We need to focus on what's important."

My mind whirs, trying to understand what this person is asking of me. He is asking impossible things.

"That is not fair! I'm *twelve*! I didn't get in a car! I didn't drink anything! I cannot fix this for you. I cannot fight dragons. I can't even keep my friends!"

I take a breath. I am scared and sad and overwhelmed and failing at being in this world. But I am Princess Auden of Sorrowfeld. I am. Even if I'm not perfect at being that either. "I know it's disappointing for everyone, but I'm just—I'm just me." I take a breath. "I want to just be a kid in a play. I want to go to rehearsal. I deserve that. I deserve something for me."

I'd missed my princess voice, which is low and steady. I finally, finally found it. It was right there, folded up in the truth.

I am glad it has returned.

Denny's dad does not know what to do with it. He opens his eyes wide, then his mouth, then closes both, then shakes his head. He does not say it is okay to go.

But he doesn't stop me when I leave.

The Tale of Dragons True

Denny, age 11

The Lake of Leer must be avoided. The Lake of Leer can turn an unsuspecting human into a dragon. If a human falls in, they will turn immediately into a dragon, tortured forever by having to leave behind their human lives.

Sometimes

in terrible circumstances

that must be avoided

a human might get

pushed

in.

Chapter 27

Denny Greene

I've read so much of *The Tale of Dragons True* lately that my eyes are tired, and passages from it ring in my head like a song that plays everywhere all summer long and always echoes in your ears. Lady Genevive lingers around me, waiting for me to come up with a way out of the moment we're in.

Runa's words are vague, but they call to me to be powerful and brave, even if she meant something different by it. She said twelve mattered, and I want to show her that it does. That *I* do.

The book can't tell me exactly what to do. But it reminds me that this is our kingdom, and that I know where the answers are. I know what we have to do next. I put the book down.

"I have to go to the Lake of Leer," I say. "The

book talks about dragons being created there. Come with me. I want to find your father and maybe even mine."

There is a long pause, and I think maybe it is the truth that makes it hard for Lady Genevive to know what to say next. The truth does that to people—stops them in their tracks, makes it hard for them to find other, less true words.

Dorothy had the Yellow Brick Road, and Princess Auden has the silver path to the Lake of Leer. Back at home there's no path, no road, and I don't know what I'm supposed to follow to make things better, which is why I don't mind so much, disappearing into Sorrowfeld or Oz, where things are stranger and scarier, sort of, but also simpler.

Find the wizard, get sent home.

Defeat the dragons, save the kingdom.

"I guess we should get you dressed for a meeting with a witch, then," Lady Genevive says at last, and I hear a strange mix of dread and hope and hatred in her voice.

"I'm dressed," I say, but my blue gown isn't right, apparently. Lady Genevive finds a gray frock that is stiff and lace-trimmed and heavy. Serious. The tiara she chooses, too, is one with gravitas—it is large and solid and studded with sapphires as big as my eyes.

She looks me over in this new costume, one that I guess is fit for a witch. "You're sure?" she asks.

"No, of course not," I say.

"Oh."

I wonder if the real Princess Auden is always certain. Based on the way Lady Genevive seems to spin from my answer, I'd say she must be. I'd like to meet this Princess Auden, who looks like me but is sturdier, wiser, more sure about what to do and how to do it. It feels strange to make up a world but not know how, exactly, to exist in it.

"I'll come," Lady Genevive says. "Maybe he's there. Maybe we'll find him."

"Maybe," I say.

The walk to the witch's house is long but clear. I pack *The Tale of Dragons True* in a parcel clearly not meant for a princess to carry. I know I'll need it, and it makes me feel closer to Runa to have it with me. We follow a series of silver bridges that cross over tiny rivers and streams and bits of forest. After nearly two hours, the witch's castle appears before us, and it is grand and familiar, stunning and mine.

I drew the castle, and Runa colored it in. I drew spires and statues and long, narrow windows and large padlocked doors. I drew pointed towers and lopsided wings, all of which Runa had colored in silver and gray and gold and a terrible deep, dark purple.

"Wow. It really looks like that," I say, wishing Runa could be here, wishing she could see what we made.

"Of course it does, we're here every year for the Witch's Wander," Lady Genevive says.

In a flash, I remember. Runa came up with the idea for the Witch's Wander when we realized we didn't know much about the witch of Sorrowfeld, except that she maybe had something to do with the dragons.

Runa said every year there should be a holiday where the whole kingdom goes to the castle and the surrounding area to look for the witch, and that anyone who finds her gets to ask for one favor. "Like hardcore hide-and-seek, where it really matters how well you seek." I remember Runa's eyebrows dancing. I remember the way her voice used to get breathy when she was excited.

"Right," I say to Lady Genevive. "The Witch's Wander. Of course."

"My father won it once," she says. "I never found out what favor he asked for." She sounds so sad, missing her dad, wishing she were in the time before this time, when things were simpler, when she really believed I might save Sorrowfeld from every threat.

If I ever get to go back to Magnolia Bend, I'll write

that kind of kingdom. Where everything is fine all the time. Where princesses don't have to make big decisions or fight battles or save anyone.

When we first wrote Sorrowfeld, it was all elegant parties and twirling dresses.

I don't know when exactly it changed, or why. Did Runa write the first scary bit, or did I? Did princesses and mermaids turn boring, or was it too sad, maybe, to write a perfect world when ours wasn't anymore?

Neither Genevive nor I is making a move toward the castle yet, both of us just staring at its imposing size and shape. So I open *The Tale of Dragons True* and flip through it, trying to parse who wrote what, when the game changed from fantastical to frightening.

Runa and I wrote about the terrible witch and her cursed lake, the way she watches people fall in, people she could save from their dragon fate. We wrote that she chooses not to help, that she lures them in, even, that she wants more dragons to do her bidding, to protect her castle, to rage against humanity.

We never wrote why.

Runa and I forgot about why a lot, it seems.

Maybe I am writing the why right now. I don't know.

But it's time to meet the witch.

I go first. I walk us around the Lake of Leer on a narrow path, careful not to lose my step and slip into the water. And in minutes we are at the witch's front door. And maybe other people, other princesses, would take a breath before knocking, would mark the momentous occasion, the enormous risk.

But I knock right away, because if I don't, I never will.

I try to stand up straight at the door. Princesses stand up straight. They take up space. They know the right way to do things. I try to be Princess Auden of Sorrowfeld.

I try and I try and I try.

But when the witch appears, I'm just Denny again.

Chapter 28

Denny Greene

The witch is not like any witch I know.

That's not right. I don't know any witches.

She is not like any witch I've imagined, a fact that can't be right, because didn't I write this one? The witch at the Lake of Leer? Maybe it was Runa who put the final touches on her. Or most likely, it seems, Runa and I wrote the bare bones of the idea of a witch and a castle and a dragon-turning lake, but we never wrote any of the details.

"Oh!" I say, surprised at the size of the witch—my size, practically—and the age of her, which seems pretty close to my age too. She's cute, a word I didn't know could be applied to witches, with blond ringlets and pink lips and rosy cheeks.

I would have drawn her green and old. I would

have made her tall and bony. I would have dressed her in black.

She's in a yellow dress with silver polka dots and purple flowers in her hair. She looks more like a fairy than a witch, except she doesn't have wings and she has the grumpy expression of someone just woken up from a stupendous nap.

"Yes?" she says. Her voice is small and airy. For a breath, she looks exactly like Sadie from back home. She has the same heart-shaped face, the same pale peach skin and light blue eyes. But in another flash, she is not Sadie at all. I am forgetting, quickly, who Sadie even is.

"We're looking for my father," Lady Genevive says before I can say anything. I don't think I've ever heard her speak first. But she's doing it now, with her arms over her chest and her chin hiked up like it might make her seem taller.

"Okay," the witch says. She blinks, waiting for more. This, too, reminds me of Sadie, who has a habit of giving me long looks after I've said the wrong thing, like she's expecting me to correct myself somehow.

"The dragons took him," I explain.

"I'm not a dragon." The witch sort of gestures to herself, as if to draw attention to her lack of tail and scales and fiery breath.

"But you have the lake," I say.

"I do."

"And the lake makes dragons," I say. Next to me, Lady Genevive shakes her head. She still believes what her father told her. That that part of the book is a lie, that dragons are only dragons, that humans can't be turned into them. I'm still trying to understand why they believe some parts and not others. Do they pretend away the scariest parts?

"It does make dragons. Yes."

Lady Genevive scoffs, unbelieving. But I ignore her.

"Because you enchanted it to." It's a strange not-conversation, where I'm just listing a bunch of facts that she obviously already knows.

"That's true."

"Well, we're here for answers."

"It sounds like you already have them." The witch tosses her hair, and she's Sadie again, impossibly cool and unreachable. "What did you say your name was?" She squints, and there's something new in her face, a bit of confusion that wasn't there a moment ago.

"Auden," I say. I don't say *Denny* and I don't say *princess*. I want to answer as close to truthfully as possible without exposing my biggest secret.

Lady Genevive's face pinches, and she corrects me, "*Princess* Auden."

"But you're not a princess," the witch says. Her eyes are more hazel than blue, I realize, and they are looking right at me—hard, if a look can have a texture, have a weight of impact.

"She's Princess Auden. The last remaining princess of Sorrowfeld," Lady Genevive says. "She just turned twelve. She's our only princess."

"No," the witch says. She shakes her head, and I don't know how she knows, but she knows. "No, she's not."

I take a step back, and then another, and my feet start to slip on the curve of the land. The castle is so close to the Lake of Leer that even the smallest misstep could land me in its waters, and my breath catches in my throat at the realization that I am slipping. I reach out for Lady Genevive, who slips as well, and in our scramble to right ourselves, we fall onto our sides, our legs, and my toe touches the top of the lake. I dig my nails into the ground and pull myself upright, trying to pretend away the feeling of the water on my left toe, trying to pretend it didn't happen at all.

The witch is unmoved. Cold. As if she's seen a hundred humans fall in and doesn't care much about any of them. She cares about whether I'm a princess, though, tilting her head as if looking for something very particular about me. She looks at Lady Genevive too. "You don't believe in the lake, but you're scared to fall in?" she asks.

Lady Genevive doesn't say anything. She's shaking. So am I.

"You," the witch says. "You, the not–princess Auden, are scared. You know what can happen."

I shrug. My heart is racing. Maybe it was a mistake coming here, putting ourselves in even more danger just to speak to a witch who has no interest in helping us at all.

"You know the rules, too," the witch says. "A witch enchants a lake to do her bidding. I chose mine to create dragons. A witch must stay in her castle at all times. And a witch must answer royal questions."

I remember writing the rules. They came so easily. They meant nothing. We were eating pretzels, we were in pajamas, it was close to bedtime, we had to write quickly before Mom told us to turn off the lights.

"Exactly! So you have to answer Princess Auden's questions," Lady Genevive says. The whole of her is solid, tense. Maybe she's seeing things differently after nearly falling into the lake. I wonder who she would be, if she didn't have to be a lady.

"I don't have to," the witch says. "I only have to answer *royal* questions, isn't that right?" She looks at me like I'm supposed to explain it all right here and now, but I can't, I'm not ready, and I don't know what it would mean if I revealed everything.

I have to get out of here, away from this place where secrets are revealed.

In Sorrowfeld, I remember writing a hundred million years ago, secrets always come out.

"I don't think your dad's here anyway," I say to Lady Genevive, who is looking around sort of desperately, like someone else might come along and give the witch a talking-to. The witch's mother, maybe. The witch's teacher. Some authority figure who can set things straight, because this curly-haired, rosy-cheeked kid can't possibly be the person in charge of a terrifying castle and an enchanted lake.

"It was your idea to come here!" Lady Genevive says. "You said it was important! You said we'd figure something out! You said you'd find my father!"

"What did you say your name was?" the witch asks. She hasn't moved a single inch. She's just lingering in her doorway, not helping, but not leaving us alone, either.

"Lady Genevive."

"Genevive. Not a princess either. But a lady. Looking for a father. You are the daughter of who, exactly?"

"Duchess Dutton and Duke Verden," Lady Genevive says. Their names are crisp and elegant coming from her. She says them like they really and truly mean something.

Something changes on the witch's face. She's still our age, but she looks older. Not just older like a teenager. But *older*. A hundred years older. A thousand.

"You're looking for Duke Verden? You're saying the dragons took him?" She seems truly astonished.

"Yes, you know him? You know my dad?"

She steps away from us a hair and reaches for the door of her castle. "I don't want anything else to do with him. He got his wish after the Witch's Wander. He knows I didn't approve of what he did. You think witches don't care about right and wrong? I don't want any kin of Duke Verden here." She sounds angry, not scared, and she shoves the door shut with finality. She spoke in riddles and didn't want us to catch up.

Back home, Sadie is like this too. She makes up her mind quickly and doesn't change it. She makes impossible rules that she doesn't explain and is angry when you don't follow them. Maybe that's how Sadie has to be. Maybe that's how the witch has to be. They have secrets, both of them, things that have happened that we don't understand. I see that now.

"What does that mean?" Lady Genevive is indignant, but no one answers.

It is simply the two of us and the Lake of Leer

stretching out blue and icy before us, a whole history hidden in its depths, a truth somewhere we can't quite reach.

Lady Genevive doesn't say a word the whole walk home.

I watch the skies for dragons.

Chapter 29

Denny Greene

Upon our return, there are knights and horses crowded around our castle. There are torches lit with flames and hoisted high in the air. There are flags waving, the symbol of Sorrowfeld that Runa and I drew over winter break one year at my kitchen counter displayed prominently on the flapping silk.

Duchess Dutton rushes to the carriage, her face drawn, her hair wild.

"We hear them, they're coming. They're coming. It's over. Sorrowfeld is over." She begins to weep. "Your father said we would be fine, he said he had fixed everything, he promised me. He promised it would all work out."

"He knew how to defeat dragons?" I ask. It's the

first I've heard of anyone knowing what in the world I'm supposed to do, and not for lack of asking.

But Duchess Dutton isn't hearing me. She's crying and grabbing hold of Lady Genevive, and she's holding her close and looking at the sky.

"He promised this was the right thing and now look, look at this and he's gone and we're here and it was a mistake, it was a terrible mistake. We should have asked the witch for gold. Or to fly. Or for a whole year of summers. Not this. Not this."

"What are you talking about?" I ask. She's talking in the same sort of code as the witch, and the flapping of wings is so loud I have to yell over the noise.

"Go! Go get them! Stand up to them the way you are supposed to do." She's speaking to me now, but not in the warm, familial way she used to. She's cold, shoving me into the path of danger. Something awful catches in my throat, a feeling of loss and rage and missing that comes whenever I think of mothers and what they are supposed to be and why I can't have one the way everyone else does. Duchess Dutton wasn't my mother, exactly, and she wasn't the real Princess Auden's either, but she was the best we had, and now she's turned away from me too.

My mind thumps with the vision of my own mom—gaunt and smelling of alcohol and clicking the lock on her bedroom door closed on a day off from school when I thought we might spend it together.

Everything hurts. Another kingdom, and the same awful loss.

There's an explosion of fire in the sky from the mouth of a dragon. It's hot and bright and terrifying. And there is the castle beneath it. Exactly the way we wrote it.

The witch was where I wrote that she'd be. The lake does what I said it would. All these people keep telling me I'm wrong about everything here, but it's *mine*. I know it.

It's a place I built, a place I invented. It's my kingdom.

I'm so far away from the story we would have written.

And the fire is so hot.

But I am not surrendering my kingdom. Sorrowfeld belongs to me. Me and Runa.

I am not Princess Auden of Sorrowfeld.

I'm something so much bigger. I am Denny, who created it.

I run inside the castle, up the stairs to the tower bedroom that has become my own. I need to catch my breath. I need to be in a place where I can listen to the one person who knows how to save the kingdom.

Me.

Chapter 30

Denny Greene

They are coming for me.

The dragons, with their heavy, flapping wings and smoky breath and scales as sharp as knives, are coming for me, the way they always come for princesses.

"They can take me instead," Lady Genevive says. I jump, hearing her voice, then seeing her body next to mine. I thought she was glued to her mother's side, but she's here, and she's offering herself up. "Sorrowfeld doesn't need me. I'm not anyone, I'm not a princess." She's the scared kind of brave—her arms across her chest, her cheeks so pink they look like flowers in bloom, her legs shaking without buckling. "It's what my dad would want, I think? Or he'd want me to be brave. He'd want me to do *something*."

From our place in the tower, all I can see is smoke and swoops of green-gold dragon tails. There are cries from the townspeople—some of them beg the dragons not to take me. Some loudly declare they'd be better off without me.

"She can't save us anyway!" they say. "Take her away!"

I'm shaking now too. My stomach spiraling, my back waterfall-wet, the whole of me wishing myself somewhere else, somewhere simpler. Home.

But this is home too. Sorrowfeld. My Sorrowfeld.

I wanted a kingdom without secrets. So I have to stop keeping them.

"I'm not a princess either," I tell Lady Genevive, who is my best friend here, even though right now she doesn't like me at all. The words come out anyway, pried out of the hard wall of untruths I've been building since I arrived here. They topple, little pebbles that were also somehow integral to the whole formation.

She doesn't hear me over the roars of dragons desperate to capture the very last princess of Sorrowfeld, the one who has remained, the one they didn't take before. Me. Or the me they think I am.

"I'm not a princess," I try again, and she hears this time. The truth has to come out, it just has to. She almost ignores the words this second time—a wave starting in her hand, a dismissive *of course you are*, beginning on her lips. But something stops her. Maybe she sees me at last. Maybe she sees what she's been missing all this time.

I look like her and sound like her and stand in this tower like her and am threatened by dragons like her. But I am not her.

I am not Princess Auden of Sorrowfeld.

I'm just Denny.

And I've said it, at last. I've said it. "I'm Denny."

The Tale of Dragons True

Runa and Denny, age 7

Sometimes Sorrowfeld has to be saved.

Princesses do the saving.

They have these princess powers like

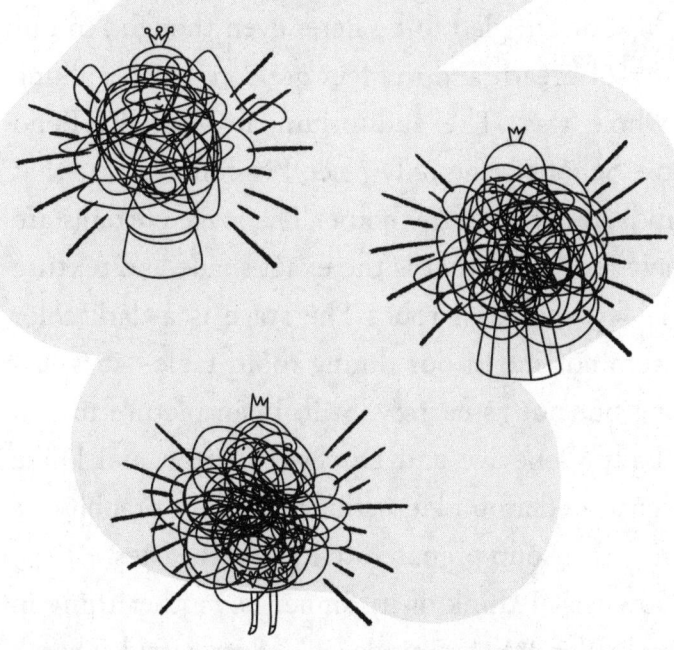

Chapter 31

Princess Auden

No one is especially happy to see me at rehearsal, but I'm glad to be here, even though I'm out of breath and my feet are sore from walking the whole way. The auditorium at Magnolia Bend Middle School is the only place I've found so far that reminds me at all of my home. The stage curtains are a heavy red velvet that is the exact shade and texture of my favorite royal robe. The stage is a dark color that reminds me of our dining room table—it is just as long but not as narrow. Still, I can picture myself and Lady Genevive and Duchess Dutton and Duke Verden seated around it, eating pheasant or rabbit or a creamy, rich soup prepared to my exact tastes.

Now that I think of it, dinner is another thing in Magnolia Bend that reminds me of Sorrowfeld. There's no pheasant or chocolate cakes with raspberry filling here, at least not in Denny's home, but there's the same quiet, the same sense that something is missing. Duchess Dutton is always trying to fill up the space, just like Denny's dad does, but it never works, and Duke Verden usually wanders off, mumbling something about work to do, even though the rest of us are still eating.

The memory hurts. I wonder if Denny is remembering her family too, if her heart aches the same way at the sadnesses left behind, the ones that feel especially hard to understand.

"Denny, I was told you weren't coming," Mr. Lowen says. He looks harried, like he's been rushing around all day, worrying. And I guess maybe he has. We have different ideas about who Dorothy is, but Mr. Lowen cares about the play just as much as the rest of us do.

"Not coming?" For a moment I think he somehow heard what happened with my mother, but I see Runa behind him and she's looking at the ground, guilty and ashamed. And next to her is Sadie.

"That's what Runa said. That you had family things going on. But if you're here—well, that changes things, doesn't it?"

"It does," I say.

Sadie still hasn't seen me, but Runa meets my gaze. She flushes. It's not an apology, but it's an acknowledgment. She nudges Sadie, whose face startles, then grimaces.

"I'm here," I say, straightening my back even more. "I'm ready."

I rehearse the show the way Mr. Lowen wants. "You're just like Judy today," he says. And even though he's spent three weeks telling us all about Judy Garland, who sort of sounds like a princess to me, I still wonder why it is a compliment in Magnolia Bend to be doing something the way someone else would.

But I do it the way he wants me to, the way someone else before me did, because I can't risk doing it any other way, not with Sadie still standing around with her hair braided, mouthing along with all my lines. Not with Denny's parents wanting me to quit the play anyway. Not with everything falling apart here in this life that isn't even my life but that I've managed to destroy anyway.

I play Dorothy as scared and meek, shuddering at every step on the Yellow Brick Road. I make my body smaller, I make my voice breathier, I tuck my hair behind my ears a million times, and I keep a hand over my heart most of the show.

Today's Dorothy is sweet and shaky and definitely loveable. I know because Mr. Lowen gives me a standing ovation, gives it to all of us, really, but he locks eyes with me and gives a double thumbs-up and bounces his knees a little, like this is everything he's ever wanted it to be.

"Finally," Sadie says on our way out the door. It should feel like an accomplishment: I'm finally a normal girl following normal girl rules, fitting in. But behind her is Runa, who looks confused about what she's supposed to say and maybe even what she's supposed to feel.

We stare at each other, and I can see that underneath everything, Runa cares about Denny, and Denny cares about Runa, but Sadie has cast some sort of spell to make that not matter as much as it should.

"What's so great about her?" I ask. "She's just a really good friend or something? She's so nice or really fun or—what is it?"

"I don't know what you're talking about."

"I'm talking about Sadie. She must be pretty great for you to do all that for her. To say I'm not coming to rehearsal. To say it's because of my family." My voice starts to shake. I was so strong a second ago, but that one word, *family*, makes me feel not strong at all.

"She is." The words are solid, but the way Runa says them isn't. "She's— Everyone likes Sadie."

"I don't."

I'm sort of stunned to say it, and Runa is definitely stunned to hear it.

"Well, that's because of, you know, how you are."

"How am I?"

"Kind of, you know, babyish. Obsessed with princesses and dragons still, even though that's sort of over."

I wonder what the real Denny would say. Or how she would feel. I wonder if she would have seen it coming, if it would have made sense to her. It doesn't make much sense to me. Of all the things I feel as Denny, babyish is not one of them. It is not babyish to listen to the sound of sirens and see your mom, crying, taken away in an ambulance. It is not babyish to have your dad look at you like you can somehow fix everything. It's not babyish to have to figure out Magnolia Bend on your own, while your best friend chooses someone else to be best friends with.

And dragons. They aren't babyish either.

"You think it's babyish because you don't think it's real," I say. I don't really mean to, I'm just tired of the way Runa is looking at me like she's better than me, like she knows something that I don't.

"And you think it *is* real?" Runa asks. She lowers her voice. "Denny. Don't say that kind of thing. Okay? People will think— You just can't talk that way."

I can tell from the way she whispers, from the

all-of-a-sudden gentleness of her tone that somehow this is Runa protecting me, this is Runa feeling she's doing me a favor.

"I'm not Denny," I whisper back. "I'm not. I'm Princess Auden. The last remaining princess of Sorrowfeld. And I need to get back."

Runa looks around to see who has heard. "Denny. Come on. We're twelve now. We can't do a whole imaginary—"

"Princess Auden," I interrupt. "It's Princess Auden. I don't know where Denny is. But if I were to guess, she's in Sorrowfeld trying to battle a dragon that only a real princess can defeat. Is she a real princess?"

It feels so good to tell the truth. My heartbeat evens out, my arms know how to move, my hands know where to land.

I can breathe.

"Denny," Runa says again. There's worry and rush, but confusion too. Wonder. She tilts her head like a new angle might help her see what I need her to see.

And maybe it does.

"Come on, Runa, my mom said she'd take us all out for sundaes." Sadie comes back into the auditorium, reaching out for Runa's hand, which finds hers easily, comfortably. The way best friends always find each other.

"Sorry, Denny. There's no room for you. But, you know, you're a princess, so I'm sure you wouldn't want to come with us anyway."

Sadie smirks and rolls her eyes. She must have been listening in. Maybe she expects me to be embarrassed or something, but she's the one who should feel bad, not me. I'm Princess Auden. I'm doing my best to be Denny, too. And all I've done is tell the truth.

"No," I say. "You're right. I wouldn't want to come at all."

Chapter 32

Princess Auden

Denny's dad isn't home when I get home. And he isn't home an hour later, when it's getting close to dinnertime. And he isn't home after I've eaten two bowls of cereal and a peanut butter and jelly sandwich, two Magnolia Bend delicacies I will dearly miss, should I ever return to Sorrowfeld.

It's bedtime when he gets back, his car grumbling along the gravel in the driveway, his steps heavy up our front steps. He doesn't call my name after he opens the door. Doesn't come looking for me upstairs. Eventually, when I realize he isn't going to find me, I find him.

"Hello," I say. "You're here."

"Oh!" His shoulders jump. His hand flies to his

chest. "Oh, Denny. You surprised me. I figured you'd have put yourself to bed."

"You didn't say you'd be gone so long."

"I had to be with Mom, honey. They're moving her into a new place, where she can get the help she needs. It was a big decision, and she needed me to help her through it. She'll be gone for a month or so. You're so independent, I knew you'd be able to handle it."

I wonder what *independent* is code for.

I wonder why he is so sure that Mom is the only one who needs him.

"Yeah," I say, though, instead of asking him. "What happens now?"

Denny's dad doesn't answer. He makes himself his own sandwich and sighs like it's a lot of work to do even that. I don't think there is an answer. He doesn't know what's going to happen next, and neither do I. Somewhere far away in Sorrowfeld, there are dragons and the girl who invented dragons, trying to battle each other. And here in Magnolia Bend, there's a sick mom and lost friends and a princess who doesn't know anything, really, about moms or friends.

"When you were little, Mom used to make you sandwiches cut into heart shapes and star shapes. She used to make peanut butter and jelly cookies. We all three used to stay up late so that we could go outside and look at constellations, and you'd fall asleep on a picnic blanket on the lawn. You remember any of that?"

"Sort of," I say, because I don't have those memories exactly, but I remember being littler and lying on the castle lawn, looking at those same constellations with Lady Genevive and Duchess Dutton. Duke Verden was never around for those times, and it was sort of nice not to have him there, reminding us of all the rules we had to follow to be the best royalty we could be. We were a princess and a lady, but we were mostly just kids, counting stars, eating grapes, not even remembering other kingdoms existed. We laughed so hard at absolutely nothing that our bellies hurt and there were no dragons in the sky. I remember falling asleep out there and waking up in the morning in my bed, not even sure how I got from one place to the other. I remember it felt like it would last forever. "I wish I were little again."

"Me too," Denny's dad says, and I've never heard a grown-up say such a thing, so it startles my heart.

I know what I need, and maybe it's what he needs too. Maybe the thing we need is actually the same.

"Can we do that tonight? Just be little again?" I ask.

I can see he's about to say no. He's tired and I'm tired and I'm mad, too, at how many times he asks me and asks Denny to fix something it isn't our job to fix. But the night is the right shade of dark and cool. The stars are bright. Denny's mom is somewhere safe, for the moment. She isn't upstairs asking us to fix something we can't fix. His no shifts to a yes. He nods.

Outside the ground is a little wet, but we don't care. We lie down on it and don't think about dirt or dew or chill or anything, really, except the stars and the moon and the impossible quiet of night, the way it makes everything seem like it might be okay.

"You're coming to the show next week, right?" I ask. I want to believe in Denny's dad, in things getting better for real.

"The show?" He sounds as if he's truly forgotten. It hurts. It is a spiky shock of hurt. "Oh, right, gosh, Den, I'll try, okay? I'll try. We'll have to see how Mom's doing, of course. But I'll try."

My whole body tenses up in response. I know how much Denny has given up, how many times she's said she doesn't need something, how often she's probably done what her parents ask of her. And I can hear in her dad's voice how used to that he is, how little she asks in return.

And I hate it.

She made a beautiful, imperfect kingdom and filled it with dragons, and she preferred to spend time there instead of here, on the lawn, with her dad. And I can't even blame her. She is so small here.

But I'm not small. I've never been small and quiet. And this, finally, is something I can do for Denny.

"No," I say, as clear as I can, the way a princess says no. "Trying isn't enough."

Denny's dad looks unsure how to respond. He lowers his head, looking like a person who will disappoint me.

But of course, he already has, so many times. There are so many things we can't fix, Denny's dad and I. But he can do more than try. He can be there. He can show up.

And that's all Denny and I can do too, really. Show up. As ourselves.

We are twelve. We can be brave and bold and kind and true. We can do math equations and fight dragons and rule kingdoms, even. But we cannot fix the way sadness sometimes settles and sticks in someone we love. We cannot make something lost return. We cannot change the way things are, we can only find ourselves, over and over again, within that mess.

Even when we switch places, switch kingdoms, switch lives and problems and worlds—we cannot switch ourselves. I wish Denny's dad would listen to me, the way the people of Sorrowfeld are told to, the way a princess is supposed to be listened to.

I am Princess Auden. She is Denny. We are twelve. We are doing our best.

I wish I could write it differently, twelve.

I have the thought, and the thought feels like an answer.

There is no book of being twelve.

But there is a book.

There is a book.

There is a book, and when it is written in, the words appear in Sorrowfeld. And the words become true.

"I can fix it," I say, so stunned that the words come out of my mouth instead of staying inside my head.

"Of course you can," Denny's dad says, sounding confused but still trying to be supportive, I guess. "You're Denny. You can do anything."

This, at least, is true. I can do anything. I have to do anything and everything that I can.

"I have to go to the shed," I say. I don't wait to see what Denny's dad feels about that. It doesn't matter. I know what I need. I know what I feel. I know what's true.

In the shed, I open *The Tale of Dragons True*. It is still a shock to see the words I know in a kid's handwriting, to see scratch-outs and rewrites and hot chocolate and Cheetos stains.

And blank pages. So many blank pages. I flip to them, passing by a list that had recently appeared in my version of the book in Sorrowfeld. It was a strange list that made no sense in the kingdom. But now that I have lived here, I see that it was a list not meant for this book. It is in the handwriting I now know to be Runa's, and it is so clearly a list of what their birthday party would be. It is the only time that their real life made it into the book, and it was about the very day that we switched places.

My heart beats fast and then faster, the way it does when something starts to make sense, even if the sense it makes is overwhelming and impossible and frightening.

The worlds collided, Magnolia Bend's concerns sneaking into Sorrowfeld's rules with just this short list that meant nothing, probably, to Runa. But it was wrong to write it here. It was wrong to let one world seep into the other. And now here I am.

I take a pen. I'm not making Runa's same mistake; I'm fixing it. I'm writing a new rule.

If a princess is banished unexpectedly to a faraway kingdom, she must find herself again. When she recalls who she is, when she is her truest self, she will be returned to whatever kingdom she calls home.

I close my eyes. "I'm Princess Auden, I'm Princess Auden," I say, waiting for us to switch back.

But nothing happens.

Absolutely nothing.

Chapter 33

Princess Auden

Days pass, and I am still here. I wrote the new rule into the old book. I was myself, I looked at the sky and said my own name. It didn't work.

I'm still here. I'm disappointed, but there is also a part of me that is relieved to not miss opening night.

If I ever return to Sorrowfeld, I think I'd like to start performing in plays. I can't return to life as a princess and just never feel this way again—buzzy and warm from lights and sticky from makeup and entirely alive. It's glorious backstage—everyone running around, talking about who is coming to see the show, practicing tricky parts of songs, tongue twisters, high notes, dance moves. Everything backstage smells like hairspray and sweat, and somehow it is a good smell, a new one, certainly—in Sorrowfeld there is no such thing as hairspray, and even the mention of sweat would be shunned by royalty, seen as untoward.

I like that here in Magnolia Bend we all get ready for the performance together, gathering around two smudged mirrors, sharing bobby pins and blush and tips for how to apply lipstick, tie a perfect bow, take a photograph that can fit six people in it. I like that I'm part of it and not somehow above it, tucked into a tower, treated with respect that sometimes feels almost like disdain or distance.

"Break a leg, Denny," the girl I've seen in the cat ear headband says. She's one of the only people who hasn't gotten the message to ignore me.

"You too," I say. The buzz in the air is so thick it's hard to even hear myself think.

I ignore Sadie, who is delicately applying mascara and singing scales, and I check my phone for the hundredth time to see if Denny's dad has texted. I want him and Denny's mom to be in the audience. I want that for her, and for me too. I didn't come all the way here to not get to have a taste of being a regular girl, a kid with two well parents sitting in the front row with bouquets of flowers like other parents.

I don't see Denny's parents, but I see Sadie's. Her mom looks excited, but her dad has his arms crossed, like he's ready to be disappointed in whatever is about to happen. I know it, because it's a look Duke Verden often has, and it's a look that feels terrible when it's directed at you.

Sadie must see that look a lot. Runa said everyone likes Sadie, and that's true at school, but for a moment I can see that even though everyone at school likes Sadie, maybe she doesn't always feel so liked, after all.

Still, her parents are here. And that's something.

Denny's mom is in that new hospital, the special kind for people who need the type of help she needs, people with bottles on the bedside tables and cars with broken doors, and kids who miss them. Denny's dad says there's visiting hours and nightly phone calls, and that sounds fine and also like even more things that Denny's mom needs that will make it hard for her parents to remember what Denny needs.

But Denny's dad could come. He *should* come. He's right down the street. No dragon has flown him into the sky, even if the disease Denny's mom has feels like a dragon sometimes, even if it feels like a burning-down castle.

I wish he could see that he is not a stolen-away king, he is not trapped in some dragon lair waiting for a princess to claim victory. He's a dad. He could just be a dad, even when it's hard.

I told him he needed to do more than try. I told him

what I saw that was wrong, but I guess he didn't listen, not really.

Mr. Lowen is rushing through the backstage area calling, "Five minutes to curtain!" a phrase that makes everyone straighten their backs, inhale sharply, shake out their nervous fingers.

Sadie seems the most scared.

I'm a different kind of scared. Because it doesn't matter what I said to Denny's dad the other day about trying. He's worried about the list of things he has to do with Denny's mom gone for a month, the work of taking care of her, even now, when a whole hospital of people are there to watch over her. Denny's dad isn't coming.

"Denny. Do it just like yesterday, okay? Yesterday was perfect. You were perfect. You finally got what I wanted. Our own Judy Garland." Mr. Lowen has found me now, and even though he's supposed to be in charge, he's not exactly calm. He's shifting his weight and talking so fast I have to ask him to slow down, which he doesn't seem entirely capable of actually doing.

I nod. It doesn't feel good.

"I love you playing with her fear. Her uncertainty. That's what we want to see from Dorothy. Lovely."

I nod again. It feels even worse.

Mr. Lowen rushes off, and I try to quiet my brain so I can focus on what I need to do, but it is rushing through a compare-and-contrast list of Magnolia Bend and Sorrowfeld, and it's finding that Magnolia Bend has more things made from fleece, more pinging phone sounds, more fraught friendships, more things that smell like weird metal versions of the things they say they're going to smell like—apple shampoo that smells like metallic apple, rose soap that smells like antiseptic roses, berry medicine that smells and tastes like only the sweetest, headachiest part of a berry.

But also.

The list in my head is revealing that in both places a few things are true: Men with beards and fast words are going to tell you who to be. Twelve is an age where you are supposed to stop being a kid, even though you are definitely still a kid. Your parents might not be there, even if everyone else's are.

There is a hush backstage as the lights dim and the audience claps. There is so much about this place I don't like and don't understand—the sound of cars on the road and the phones in everyone's hands and the way Denny has a mom but also sort of doesn't, how Denny maybe sort of *is* the mom, except is also not in charge of anything. Denny's life is filled with two opposite things that are both supposed to be true. But what I hate most of all is that Denny is supposed to be small and quiet and unwanting, unasking. And if she isn't, she loses everything.

There is so much about Denny's life I don't like and don't understand, but this, this moment before the show begins, I think I love. My chest is pounding and my feet are sweating, but I am also vibrating with hereness, with bigness, with readiness.

The first chords play, and I step onstage, where it is hot and bright and beautiful.

I have failed a hundred times at being Denny.

And according to Mr. Lowen, I'm usually not so great at being Dorothy either.

I wrote one rule in *The Tale of Dragons True*. There is only one way home. For Dorothy. For Denny. For me. The way home is in being my true self. Is in locating that self in this unlikeliest place.

And here I am—sweaty and lit up and excited and terrified.

I let myself look at the audience once again, just in case, even though I know he's not here, I know I bungled it all, I know I ruined everything.

Except.

The door opens, a crack of light shines through, interrupting the blackness over the audience.

And there, in the crack of light interrupting the darkness, is Denny's dad.

Who listened to me. Who did more than try. Who heard the things I said.

I am Princess Auden of Sorrowfeld. I am big and brave, and I say things and people listen. I am Princess Auden of Sorrowfeld, and maybe I can't defeat a dragon or save a mother, but I can do something, I did *something*.

I dig my heels down into the stage and tilt my chin up into the light, and I let my voice be strong and big and in charge. I am brave and bold and powerful on that stage, from the first moments of being on the farm with Aunt Em, to clicking my heels and saying *there's no place like home, there's no place like home,* because I know, finally, that it's true: there isn't. Dorothy doesn't say home is perfect or always fun or easy. She says there's no place like it. She says it's where she needs to be.

In the audience, I bet Denny's dad is beaming.

Maybe there are dragons waiting for me. Or a ruined kingdom. Or a victorious Denny who has fixed everything. I don't know. I can't know. But I sing louder and stronger and braver than I ever have. I am Princess Auden, the last remaining princess of Sorrowfeld. I have a destiny. I have a job to do.

And finally, finally, I know how to do it.

I close my eyes for the final note of the show. I close them for longer than a blink.

It takes a long time for me to open them again.

The Tale of Dragons True

Princess Auden, age 12

If a princess is banished unexpectedly to a faraway kingdom, she must find herself again. When she recalls who she is, when she is her truest self, she will be returned to whatever kingdom she calls home.

Chapter 34

Denny Greene

"No," Lady Genevive says. "You are Princess Auden."

"I'm Denny," I say again. "The witch knew. She didn't answer my questions. She knew I wasn't a princess. And these dragons know too. I'm not a princess. We look the same, but everything else— I've been here since my birthday. Her birthday. Our birthday. Aren't I different than— Aren't I someone else? Can't you tell?"

I want Lady Genevive to know the difference. I want to know that Runa would see the difference too. Wouldn't everyone? Shouldn't they all know I'm someone else, even if I look like her? In Magnolia Bend, do they all think the princess is me? Can they not see past the thick bangs and heart birthmark and wide eyes?

Lady Genevive is quiet a long time. I see her calculating the days that have passed, the things that have happened since I arrived. She's putting together a jigsaw puzzle, and finally the pieces are fitting. It's a different picture entirely than the one promised on the box.

"I woke up outside the castle, everyone freaking out about dragons. I thought I could figure it out— I thought I understood Sorrowfeld. But everything that has happened since that moment— Can't you see it? Wouldn't the real princess have known what to do? Wouldn't she have saved your father, saved the kingdom, figured it all out? Haven't I been different since then? Can't you tell?"

Lady Genevive squints. She closes her eyes. I think she is going through what has happened and how it has felt and the wrongness of these weeks. I watch her shoulders go up and down. Something in her calms. Not because everything's okay, but because finally, finally, everything makes sense.

She opens her eyes again, and they fill with tears— the truth suddenly clear and disrupting and unshakable.

"You look just like her," she says. "But you're not her."

"Do you think she's in Magnolia Bend?" I ask. It's the question I've been wondering since I arrived practically, and it feels good to finally ask it.

"That's your kingdom?"

"It's just a town." I want to explain the way houses there look—square and towerless and made of brick or wood but never stone. I want to tell her I'm not a princess there, I'm not anyone, really. I'm Runa's best friend and Mom and Dad's good daughter, but I'm not sure I'm those things anymore either.

But there's no time to tell Lady Genevive any of that. There's a burst of fire outside the biggest window. It reminds me of watching thunderstorms from the living room window with Mom. I hate thunder, and she used to hold me while we watched the rain pour, listening to the sounds that at the time were the loudest thing I could imagine. I'd never heard dragon wings then. I'd never heard their roars.

Except I'd heard them in my head. In my heart. I'd invented them, hadn't I? They're mine, aren't they?

I take Lady Genevive's hand. She startles, then lets her hand sink into the hold.

"They're so big," she says. "They're so scary."

There is one that is flying close to the window. She is smaller than the others, with brilliant gold scales and silver eyes. Her tail looks like it has been dipped in glitter, and fire pours from her mouth.

"They're beautiful," I say.

At the next burst of flame, Lady Genevive looks away. But I don't.

Mom used to tell me that hiding from the storms would only make them scarier. She would tell me to look at the patterns the raindrops made on the window and to imagine the sound of the thunder as the skies grumbling, the look of lightning as a wink from the universe. She'd take out the softest blankets, and we'd wrap ourselves in those. They were storm blankets; we didn't use them any other time. So little by little, I started hoping for storms. So that we could have the blankets and the time on the couch up past bedtime and the sound of Mom describing the world in new ways to me.

I keep looking at that dragon. She dances in the sky.

"You're so beautiful," I say to her. "That's such a beautiful dance."

Lady Genevive is crying, and the people of the kingdom are running out the gates, they are throwing stones at the beasts in the sky, they are screaming words so cruel even the meanest sixth graders at school wouldn't say them.

But I just watch the dragon and try to remember what Runa and I wrote in our book about them. We wrote this world. We wrote these beings.

Dragons aren't scared of stones and screams. They aren't scared of storms either. They're scared of the lives they left behind.

Dragons are just humans who don't get to be humans anymore.

My heart flips and my stomach slips and a feeling of worry and wonder rises up up up in my chest.

These dragons keep swarming the kingdom, circling the castle. A burst of flame takes out the East Tower. An attack, the first one, and I'm scared, but I know, I *know* it's because they are sad and getting sadder still. Another one burns the lawn, the gardens, the bridge over the moat.

Dragons are just beings who miss the life they once led.

I open the window, and Lady Genevive screams. She throws herself across the room, begging me to close it again. I love Lady Genevive. But she doesn't know what it is to miss the imperfect place you were taken from. She doesn't know about the anger of letting go, the sadness of saying goodbye to the ways things used to be.

The dragons know. And so do I.

"I miss home," I say to the sky, but also to the closest dragon, the young one, with her wings that look like they're made of sunlight. "I miss home the way it was when I was taken, but I miss the other home too. The one when I was younger. I miss being seven and watching storms with my mom. I miss being eight and having a birthday party with Runa where I could wear what I wanted and no one cared. I miss Mom waking up before me to get ready for work and I miss Dad cracking jokes about her crazy outfits and I miss talking about dragons and not crushes and not bras and not periods and not how Mom is doing and whether I can fix her. I miss my bedroom and the kitchen counter and the corner in the school library where no one can see you and you can read in peace and quiet if you need a break. I miss it so much I don't even want to think about it sometimes. I miss lemonade stands and going too high on the swings and when Mom used to read me fairy tales before bed. I miss so much. It makes me angry, too. All the things there are to miss."

I'm so caught up in making the list of things I miss, in remembering the shapes of the objects in my home and the way it used to feel to live in it, that I don't notice the dragon has stopped breathing fire. But when I catch my breath, I see that her wings have slowed, she is practically just floating in the sky now, hovering right outside the window.

We make eye contact.

I've never looked a dragon in the eyes before. Duchess Dutton said not to. The list of rules written on the library chalkboard by Duke Verden was very clear on that.

But that is not a rule we wrote in *The Tale of Dragons True*.

That is one of Duke Verden's rules. And I'm not sure that his rules are ones worth following.

Besides, I don't know where else to look. And maybe the dragon doesn't either. She flies closer and closer to the window.

"Look away!" Lady Genevive cries, but that's all we've ever done with the dragons; we've only ever looked away, and still they're here and still no magical solution for how to rid the kingdom has occurred to me, the last remaining princess of Sorrowfeld, or at least a person pretending to be that person.

I look and look and look, and the dragon looks back, and in the dragon's eyes, something forms. It is unfamiliar at first, because it's shining and purple and blue and green. It runs down her dragon cheek, navigating the scaly bumps. Another comes, and another.

Tears. Dragon tears, which are lovelier than I would have ever imagined, and bigger too. Like jewels streaming from her brilliant eyes.

"She's sad," I say. "You're sad."

She nods. More tears fall.

"Me too," I say.

With her flapping at the window and no longer diving through the sky, I can take in more of her. The shade of her eyes, which isn't actually silver so much as a kind of shiny blue, and the shape of her tail, which isn't as sharp as I had imagined it to be. Her scales look dull, soft even, and there's a sweetness to her face—all big eyes and sad mouth and eyelashes that bat a slow rhythm in time with her wings.

There is something else too.

It's around her neck. A gold line that nearly blends in with her golden scales, and then a dewdrop of red. I squint. She flies closer to the window like she wants me to see it too, like it's meant to tell me something.

A necklace.

A thin gold chain and a tiny ruby heart at the end.

A princess's birthstone necklace. Just the way we wrote it, except it's on a dragon.

I've seen it before.

I wrote it.

My hand finds my heart, and my fingers dig in, like the skin there is an anchor for this moment. But really there is no anchor, there is no way to be solid and still here.

I look at the other dragons farther away in the sky. Two larger ones and one small one.

A family of dragons.

Jewels around the smaller ones' necks. Birthstones.

Always circling the kingdom, visiting on the princess's birthday.

I close my eyes and remember the words we wrote,

the truths we invented. *The Tale of Dragons True.* It was real. It was all real. The cold of the castle. The weight of the crown. The smell of roses and vanilla folded into my bedding. The dragons and their fiery breath. The princesses with the birthstones around their necks.

The Lake of Leer, where a person can turn into a dragon.

The dragons we wrote—longing, grieving, desperate for their forgotten lives.

And these dragons here, who the people of Sorrowfeld have been told not to look too closely at.

Because if they looked closely, it would all look so very, very different.

"Lady Genevive," I say. "I know why the dragons are here. I know who they are."

"They're dragons," Lady Genevive says. Like just because someone is something right that moment means that's all they have ever and will ever be. But of course I know that isn't true.

"They're not just dragons," I say, and it is the truest thing I've ever said. Because no one is just one thing. No one is just a dragon. Or just a princess. Or just a girl with a sick mom and no need for a bra or a tampon or a popular group of friends, who wishes she could be an actress. "Look at her neck. The ruby necklace. The princess birthstone. You see? That's not just a dragon. That is Auden's sister. That's Princess Cassandra."

Lady Genevive shakes her head, but she sees the ruby, I know she does. I don't know how to make her understand everything I know, I don't know how to explain any of that.

But I know how to look at someone, really look at them, and really see them.

I can't convince Lady Genevive of the truth about Sorrowfeld. But I can look at the dragons. I can *show* her the truth.

Their wings flap more slowly. The whole world seems to slow down.

I wrote the book on dragons. I know about people who are one way and then another, people who are beautiful and turn ugly. I know people can be not themselves, and I believe, because I have to, that they can come back to themselves again. I know about stopping and waiting and listening and believing. I know about the tiny hope that something awful will turn good again. I know how to keep that hope alive.

It's good to be a leader, to be sure and shout orders. But I'm better at this. I'm better at watching and waiting and listening to the flap of wings and the words in my own heart, telling me that this is right.

Princess Auden, I'm sure, would take control and follow the rules of the kingdom and save the day.

But I only know what Runa and I wrote.

Dragons are just humans who don't get to be humans anymore, after falling in the Lake of Leer.

Dragons are just beings who miss the life they once led.

They're angry at what they had to give up. They want to destroy everything so they won't have to remember. They want to destroy the things that remind them of those lives.

I think of last Christmas, decorating the Christmas tree. Mom had been drinking. Dad had been pretending not to see it. I tried hanging my favorite ornaments on the tree. The clay stocking I made and sloppily painted when I was little. The shiny dragon Runa gave me the year before.

The photo of our family in a Popsicle stick frame that is supposed to go near the top.

I hung them one by one until I got to that frame. That photo. My big ears and clueless smile. Dad's goofy grin. And the version of Mom I love, the one with the laugh in her eyes and the steady hand on my shoulder and the silly Christmas sweater with jingle bells hanging from the sleeves.

I couldn't put it on the tree.

I couldn't put it back in the box.

So I tore it to pieces.

I've been a princess all these weeks. But I've been a dragon before too, so mad at the things I've lost that I have to destroy what's left behind.

Runa and I wrote both: princesses and dragons.

We've all maybe been both.

"I see you," I say through the window. "I see you."

And I'm saying it to the dragon, but I'm saying it to me, too. To everyone. I'm saying it soft and true. I close my eyes and say it one more time.

"I see you, Cassandra," I say, my eyes closed, my mouth braver than the rest of me, saying what Duke Verden said not to say, breaking all the rules he set out, because I am suddenly so sure that the dragons are not the villains of this story. If Sorrowfeld is the story that Runa and I wrote, the dragons were the heroes and the victims, but they were not the monsters, not really. The monsters were whoever cursed them to live this way.

The monsters were whoever didn't understand them.

"Cassandra," I say again, smiling at how good it feels to stop following someone else's rules and to return to the ones I wrote myself, with my best friend, in our garden shed, when we were tucked away somewhere safe and cozy.

Somewhere I wish I could be. Somewhere I belong.

Chapter 35

Princess Auden

The one thing I was told never to do, not ever, no matter what, was to look directly at a dragon. It's the last thing Duke Verden said to me before I ran out of my birthday party, before my whole world turned upside down.

That rule seemed real, seemed true and easy enough to follow. I didn't want to look at dragons, I didn't like their silver eyes, their sharp scales, the heavy flap of their wings.

But when I open my eyes, I am looking at a dragon.

I am looking at a dragon in Sorrowfeld. I am here, I am here, I am here.

I gasp at the bigness of it. I am in a tower. There is a dragon. Our kingdom is in disarray, the stage in Magnolia Bend is gone, I am me again, but different. I am Denny too, a little. I stumble backward, but I don't look away.

Denny was looking at the dragon.

So I do it too.

I hear Lady Genevive begging at me to turn away, and I almost do. The instinct to never look a dragon in the eyes goes deep, stays strong.

But I stay. And in the staying, something happens that has never happened before, because I have never stayed before.

The dragon's tail vanishes. The green from her body fades to a pale peach color. Her shape shifts from dragon to something else and that something else, that strange in-between shape, eventually turns into a human one.

I open the window wide. I don't know if I should, but I do it anyway. She lands on the sill.

Her wings fade to nothing, and her girl body emerges. Like that, she is a girl perched on a window.

Only a princess knows how to battle a dragon, they say.

I don't know if this is what they meant.

I look at the girl, and she looks at me. It takes three long breaths to recognize each other.

"Cassandra," I say, the word feeling like an incantation.

"Auden," she whispers back.

Right behind us is Lady Genevive, and behind her

the whole castle, the whole kingdom, and three more dragons still breathing fire, still threatening destruction. But right now it's just me and Cassandra, two sisters shocked to be together.

"You— They said you were captured. They said the dragons took you. To a cave maybe. Or killed you. They said— Oh my gosh, is that Mom and Dad and Penelope? Were you all— Did you all— You're the dragons? You all are the dragons?"

My brain is a forest, a dark one, with more trees than I would have guessed existed on earth. I haven't had a moment to take in having just been Denny and now being me again. I haven't settled my body into this new reality, and now here we are, my life story rewriting itself once again.

Cassandra's brain must be made of tall trees and thick fog, too, because she is quiet and struck. Her mouth doesn't make words, but her arms pull me in, and we stay like that a long time.

When we break apart, there are hundreds of things to say, but only one thing that truly matters. She steps into the room with me.

"How did you change back into you? What happened? I wasn't— I wasn't here. What did she do? How did she save you? Why were you a dragon? I don't understand. I don't understand."

Lady Genevive is frozen. I feel a surge of love for Denny, for whatever she did. And then a heated shame for all I was unable to do. She brought my family back to me. I took her friends away from her. I'm returning to a dream coming true, and she's in Magnolia Bend alone. I wish I could see her, meet her, help her.

"You looked at her, even though the rules say not to," Lady Genevive says. "And then you said her name, which somehow you knew. You said all this stuff about necklaces and you—and you saved her." She looks as surprised to be speaking as I am to be listening.

I look out the window at the other three dragons flying around. "It's them?" I ask my sister, squeezing her hand in worry that she will vanish again. "It's them? It really is?"

"It's us," Cassandra says. "Look at us."

So I do. Saying their names, one after the next. "Rosemary. Penelope. Berlow."

And one by one, they shift from dragon to human, from terror to wonder. The joy of their sudden arrival is too much, and I collapse into cries and hugs and weak knees, and my head simply won't stop shaking at the impossibility of all of it.

My mother kisses my face a hundred times and my father gives me a hug that I get lost in and my sisters drape themselves all over me, touching my hair, holding my hand, pulling me close.

We are a family. We are a family again.

I practically pulse with happiness.

But only a few feet away, Lady Genevive slumps with sorrow. "And my father?" she asks, trying to be polite, trying not to interrupt the moment but finding it impossible not to. "Where might he be? Is he— Can you lead us to him?"

The joy subsides. My family members hang their heads, clasp their hands, exchange glances that mean something terrible.

"Your father, Duke Verden, brought us to the Lake of Leer," my father says in his kind but sturdy way. "It was his one wish after winning the Witch's Wander. To have time alone with us. To push us in."

My father pauses to give the words space. Lady Genevive is already shaking her head, but truths click into place in my own heart, memories of rules Duke Verden told me, rules he wrote down on papers and slipped into the back of *The Tale of Dragons True*. Amendments, interpretations, things he said he understood because of how much time he'd spent studying the enchanted text. Rules and ideas that weren't written by Denny and Runa.

I think of his warnings—to not look dragons in the

eye, to stay away from the witch. His promise that he would help me rule the kingdom. His desperation for me to defeat the dragons.

The way he told me, over and over, in a million ways, that he knew more than me about the enchanted text.

When in reality it was written in a shed in Magnolia Bend by a young girl who looks exactly like me.

"He wanted— He had great wishes for power," my mother says, taking over for my father, who looks painfully at Lady Genevive, unable to finish breaking her heart. "At any cost. He wanted to rid the world of dragons. To keep you safe. And we didn't want that. Dragons—they are complicated beings. We couldn't just dismiss them out of hand. We fought about it. And I suppose he wanted to make those decisions without us."

"So he turned you into dragons?" Lady Genevive says, her voice crackling and confused.

"When you are scared, you do strange things," Mom says. "He was scared for you. Scared of the world filled with dragons. Scared of all the difficult things to come. And he—he did something awful to try to fix it."

"But now where is he?" Lady Genevive asks again. My father puts his shoulders back. Sighs a heavy sigh. My mother puts a hand on Lady Genevive's shaking shoulder.

"We did what we felt we had to do. To give him time to understand his mistake." My father looks at my mother again, unable to say the last part.

"We brought him to the lake. We believe he will understand, after he has lived the life of a dragon." My mother swallows.

There is a deep stillness in the room. Grief and confusion and calculating the way the world works.

"He can be saved. Of course. Just like any other dragon."

"So bring him back here now. I'll look at him. I'll say his name," Lady Genevive says.

"He has to want to be seen," Mom says, as kindly as she can, "for who he truly is. His mistakes, too. He has to come back to show you himself. I expect right now, as a dragon, he probably feels quite conflicted. He hates dragons. And now— Well. But I believe he will understand, eventually. And want to be seen. And come back to work with us, and not against us. Someday, Lady Genevive."

My best friend in the world is a statue, and my mother puts an arm around her. Lady Genevive doesn't lean into it or away from it. It is too much to consider, too much to try to understand at once. Downstairs, Duchess Dutton is calling for us. We'll learn what she knew, and she'll find out what we know. She'll see my family. She'll see the open window. Maybe she heard the wings, different than the others, flapping faster, flying away. Maybe she knew it might turn out this way.

I take *The Tale of Dragons True* off the shelf. The new words I wrote are there. I hope perhaps Denny will write more rules, more histories, more stories of the ways we can make things better, more magic that we can use for good.

I don't know what exactly she learned while she was here. But I hope she writes the best world she can for us. For Sorrowfeld.

Chapter 36

Denny Greene

I brace myself for the singular view of the dragon's eyes, her sharp teeth, the never-before-seen shade of her golden scales. But when my eyes open, all I see for a long, silent moment is light. Bright white light that I lift my hand to shade my eyes from, and when I do, I see I am not in a castle and I am not near a dragon, but I am onstage looking out at a very crowded version of the Magnolia Bend Middle School auditorium and I'm Denny again, and also I am someone entirely new.

There's a burst of applause, and it's for me, but it's also not for me because I wasn't here, I wasn't playing whatever part I got after the auditions I didn't ever get to participate in.

I look at my body to see what I might be—a lion or a witch or a little Munchkin. But instead I see a blue-and-white-checkered dress, a woven basket, and a pair of glittery red shoes that, now that I am able to think about it, pinch my feet but also feel a little magical.

I'm Dorothy. I got Dorothy.

It is nearly too much to take in, and I feel unmeasurable happiness and then an immediate pang of sadness, a sort of strange longing—jealousy of the person who got the part, who is me but was not me, exactly, at the time, and I'm so caught up in the mess of feelings that I almost forget to bow, but someone is holding my hand and pulling me down, and I remember to bend at the waist and smile, and bow again, and look out at the audience in the hopes of catching sight of my parents, but I don't see them in the sea of faces.

After the sadness and happiness and jealousy and shock comes something else, which is embarrassment, except bigger. Princess Auden came into my life and got my dream role and, judging from the amount of applause, the glow of the cast, played it perfectly. And I went to her world and didn't defeat a single dragon.

I know without knowing that she is there now, facing the dragon and hopefully, somehow, coming to understand what I had come to understand and hopefully, somehow, maybe, having that knowledge lead to fixing everything. It isn't enough to know her sisters, her mom and dad, are the very dragons she's been told to destroy. She has to figure out how to get them back.

I wasn't a very good princess, and I'd apologize if I could, but I don't know how I ended up in Sorrowfeld or how I finally made my way back to Magnolia Bend. There was no Tin Man or wizard or winding yellow road to follow.

The curtain falls and the cast erupts into excitement at what we've accomplished. Kids fall into hugs, burst into cheers, jump up and down with pride and delight.

I look for Runa, my arms already a bit outstretched. She should be here, she was always planning to work tech on the show, and she must be so excited for me, finally doing the very thing she told me I'd be able to do.

I look and look until I see her. Brown hair. Round face. Dressed all in black like everyone else working backstage. But she isn't looking for me. Her arms are around someone else, their two bodies jumping up and down and squealing the way we always used to do.

The someone else is the Scarecrow, who is also Sadie, and they are zeroed in on one another so much that I don't think I should interrupt. I can see that's not where I'm meant to be anymore.

A few people I don't know well tell me how great

I was, pat my shoulder, give me a flimsy side hug. But there's no one here to share the moment with in the big way, the real way.

I undress and re-dress in the changing room, the energy so electric around me I can almost pretend I'm a part of it. But when I walk out the stage door to the lobby where parents and siblings and friends and crushes wait with bouquets of flowers, that electricity shuts down and I'm in a blackout.

There is no one waiting for me with a bunch of roses wrapped in cellophane. No Mom. No Dad. I feel unsteady, like a person who has just left a boat for the first time in weeks, months, and I'm wobbly on land. I have no idea what to do—go home, I guess? I don't know what's waiting for me there, though. Mom asleep upstairs, Dad fretting downstairs, telling me over and over again that I'm okay even when I'm not?

Or something else?

Princess Auden was here, and I've never met her, but I've been her. The sort of person who might change everything.

Like me, I guess. I'm that kind of person too, it turns out.

"You were good," a voice says. "Like, really good."

I turn to face the voice, and it's another girl dressed in black. A cat ear headband on her head. Not Runa. I recognize her vaguely but don't know her name. She's smiling and sparkly eyed, and there's warmth there, so I smile back. "I know how nervous you were. You didn't have to be. You really were great."

"Oh. Wow. Thank you." I try to take it in. I want to feel it. That someone saw me. Noticed me. Recognized me. "Thank you," I say again.

"My parents and I are going out for ice cream to celebrate. I'm sure you have a million other people wanting to see you. But if you want ice cream, you could come?"

I look around for someone to ask if it's okay, but no one is here. My phone! I almost forgot about phones. It's in my bag, right where it always is. I'll text Mom and Dad and ask if I can go. But when I look at the screen, Dad's already texted me.

YOU WERE AMAZING, he's texted. Mom's doctor needed to talk to me, and I didn't want to do that with you and take away from your big moment. And that sure was one big moment. I'm so proud of you, Den. You're a special kid.

For all the things he's said, I linger on him calling me a kid.

It feels like someone telling me to take a breath.

I don't know what the rest means, about Mom's doctor or if she watched me too or anything else, but I'm a kid. I'm a special kid.

"I'm so sorry, I'm totally spacing," I say to the girl who is maybe a new friend Princess Auden made for me. "What's your name again?"

"That's okay," the girl says. "I didn't tell you before. It's Cassandra."

My heart erupts with a sort of hope.

Cassandra. Like Princess Auden's lost-but-not-really-lost sister. It's a good name. She's got a nice laugh.

I have done braver things, lately, than go to ice cream with a new friend. I have traveled much farther than that.

So I say yes.

Chapter 37

Denny Greene

Cassandra's parents return me home and ask to say hi to my parents, but I promise that they can meet them soon, at the next show maybe, at the cast party, soon soon soon. I hope it's true.

The ice cream was almost too cold but not quite, so chocolatey I forgot Sorrowfeld for a bit. I forgot Runa too, and Mom even. A new friend and ice cream can do that sometimes—let you slip somewhere else for a moment. Not to another kingdom or anything, but just a little bit away from the things that are hard.

"Want to hang out this weekend?" Cassandra asks before I get to my front door. Cassandra has a temporary tattoo of fairy wings on the back of her hand.

Her socks are mismatched and her voice is scratchy and her parents call her Cassie-Cat and she sort of blushes when they do but doesn't tell them to stop.

"Sure," I say. I've never needed a new friend. Runa was always more than enough.

"Cool." She smiles again, that big, guileless smile, and I have a feeling we are going to be friends, the real kind.

I sort of wait on the lawn, thinking maybe Runa will come by and say something, anything, about the performance, about our friendship. I don't know what's happened in these last weeks, and more than that, I don't know, really, what happened before the switch either.

Five minutes pass. Ten. And I know Runa's not coming. She's somewhere with Sadie and Emily, and I'm here with a hundred questions about what Princess Auden did as me, and what she's doing now, and if I'll ever see Sorrowfeld, the real one, again.

"Denny?"

It's been weeks since I've seen him, even if he doesn't know that. I missed him. I throw myself into a hug, and he doesn't let go.

"You okay?" he asks in a voice that sounds new, or maybe I've just been gone a long time. Dad never asks if I'm okay, I realize. He just always assumes I am.

"It's been a lot lately," I say, which is true in a million and one ways.

"It has," he agrees, and this is new too. Him not telling me everything's fine. "But let's focus on you and your performance! You were spectacular! You're a superstar!"

My chest blossoms with something just as new as everything Dad's saying and doing. *Let's focus on you.* I feel my feet firmer on the ground. My heart more securely in my chest. I feel like a person who is here, and who matters.

"How's Mom?" I ask at last, because when he's not making me worry about her, I have the space to wonder.

"You know, she's settling in at the hospital as best she can," he says. "If she wasn't there, she'd have been at the show. I'd have made sure of that. I heard you. I really did. I have to do more than try."

I would have liked to see whatever the conversation was between Dad and Princess Auden. I wonder if he'll ever know he was admonished by Sorrowfeld royalty.

"Mom's in the hospital?" I try to make it sound like a statement, not a question, but Dad can hear my confusion, and it makes him look at me extra long.

"The car accident," he says. "Her drinking."

I nod. I can't tell him where I've been. I'm going to have to piece together what's happened here by being a sort of detective of my own life. But the words *car accident* and *drinking* are scarier than a hundred dragons, a thousand witches.

"I know it's scary," Dad says. "But I can do the worrying, okay? You need to do your show. And hang out with friends. And make your bed. The doctors and I—we'll figure out how to help Mom. Okay?"

I start to argue with him—*No, it's my job, I know how to make Mom happy, I just saved a kingdom from dragons, I just visited an entire world I made up in my head*—but he sounds sure of his words, and I definitely don't know more than doctors know, and it sounds amazing, actually, to just focus on singing and acting and making plans with Cassandra and not saving anyone from anything at all.

"Want to stay up late, watch a movie?" Dad asks.

"Really?" It's already late, and Dad is a stickler for bedtime.

"Sure, why not, you had a big day, we could both use a fun night, right? And you're twelve. About time for a midnight movie marathon, I think."

I grin.

It is the first thing about being twelve that sounds absolutely and completely wonderful.

And it is.

Chapter 38

Denny Greene

I wake up on the couch, Dad snoring on his end, me tucked under a cozy blanket on mine, the credits of the last movie of our marathon parading across the screen. It's so late that it's early morning, and the dark is just turning to light.

The color of the sun rising reminds me of Sorrowfeld, where the sky is always a golden-blue-peach, except when dragons are filling it up with smoke and fire and fear.

There is only one place I want to be on this sleepy almost-morning, as I try to understand the way the past few weeks have unwound and wound me up. I slide on slippers and a robe and sneak out to the backyard, to my garden shed, where I haven't been since the switch. It looks different, smaller and sweeter, since having been to the real Sorrowfeld. There's the dragon everything, the piles of pillows on the floor, the cup filled with markers and pens, the posters of musicals, the memories of everything I have loved, the things that are left of me and Runa.

I miss Runa the way I miss Mom—painfully, with confusion and ache and anger and a splash of hope that brightens the whole mess up a bit.

On the table in the shed are two objects. The mirror Runa gave me for my birthday that I know now is how I ended up in Sorrowfeld. I turn it over, slide it away from me. And there is *The Tale of Dragons True*, the original version. I open it up and flip through familiar pages of rules and maps and ideas that all came to be. Runa's list of party ideas that is so wrong in the midst of everything Sorrowfeld that I know it, too, was a mistake, an entryway to that other world, a mixing up of here and there that never should have been.

Then there's one page I haven't seen before. It's in handwriting that looks like mine, but curvier, prettier, more royal.

The handwriting of a princess.

If a princess is banished unexpectedly to a faraway kingdom, she must find herself again. When she recalls who she is, when she is her truest self, she will be returned to whatever kingdom she calls home.

She wrote a new rule, and the rule became true. When I was in that tower, figuring out that a dragon wasn't an evil being but a misunderstood one, I was myself, my truest self. And I was returned home.

"Thank you, Princess Auden," I whisper to the wind.

Except I don't have to whisper it to the wind. I have a book right here. And the things I write in this book show up in that tall tower, in that beautiful tower, in that world so far away and so, so incredibly close to this one.

Thank you for saving us, bringing us home. I am going to be okay, I write to Princess Auden. I'm going to just be me.

Chapter 39

Princess Auden

I'm up all night with my sisters, talking about what it felt like to be a dragon, and how it was to be the last remaining princess. They tell me about coming on my birthday every year, how they hoped I'd understand eventually. They talk over each other about this year's birthday visit, and how they knew something had changed, that a new bit of magic was in the air, and it was time for them to make themselves clearer. They talk in fearful whispers about their choice to take Duke Verden. They are shocked at the things I tell them about the other kingdom I visited, Magnolia Bend. They look to the sky and say Denny's name, and we all hope that lets her know how grateful we are for the way she understood, for the way she brought us back together.

She is the truest princess of all, we agree.

We eat chocolates and walk in circles around the castle, and we tell stories—long, awful ones and short, silly ones and rambling ones that don't go anywhere actually, to try to understand everything about these years that have passed.

We fall asleep in my bed, the three of us decidedly unprincess-like, still in our gowns and shoes and crowns draped over the coziest, silkiest, heaviest blankets Sorrowfeld has to offer. I'm on the edge of the bed and wake up with a crick in my neck and a light in my heart. Cassandra and Penelope are still asleep, breathing slow, heavy breaths that I can tell will last most of the morning. It is hard on a body, to move from princess to dragon and back again.

I sneak out of bed in that early morning light, before anyone else in the whole kingdom is awake. It smells like the night after a fire. It feels like a brand-new place to be. I wander, trying to figure out what I'm looking for, before I realize I'm looking for Denny. I don't know her and I know her so well. I miss her and I've never met her. I am her and I don't get her at all. She is the only person who would understand what I've been through.

I open up *The Tale of Dragons True*. I don't know what I'm looking for—just a reminder of Denny, I guess. And wondering if she's written a new story of Sorrowfeld. I know she will write a kingdom where families can come back together, where even the most misunderstood creatures can be loved and seen and saved.

I flip to the back of the book, and there's already something there. A new entry. A note from Denny to me. We are not the same, I know we aren't, but also we sometimes are. I touch the words and nod. She will be okay. Me too. We gave each other that.

We wrote new stories for each other.

I think of the story of finding my family again.

And I hope and hope and hope that soon she'll be able to tell the story of her family finding itself again too.

I think of the dragons in the sky, and the way they weren't what anyone thought they were.

And I know that absolutely anything can happen.

And that Denny knows how to make a story beautiful.

Even a story filled with dragons.

Acknowledgments

I want to take a moment to thank everyone who helped make this book a book, and also to acknowledge how truly thrilled I am to have been writing for young people for the last thirteen or so years. Thank you to my agent, Victoria Marini, for being around for each and every one of those years—it is a joy to do this together.

A huge thank-you to my editor, Courtney Stevenson, for your thoughtful ideas, your spirit-lifting enthusiasm, your brilliant work in helping me make the path from what I originally had on the page to what I really wanted to say—I'm so grateful to have made this book with you.

I also want to thank Mabel Hsu for your help in clarifying and bolstering this early idea and believing in my stories.

To the incredible team at Quill Tree, I am so in awe of the work you do and the dedication, precision, and heart you bring to your work. Thank you in particular to production manager Vanessa Nuttry, production editor Caitlin Lonning, designer Amy Ryan, marketing director Nicole Wills, and copyeditor Ana Deboo. I'm so proud of the book you have made into a real, actual book.

An awestruck thank-you to Matt Rockefeller for your incredible cover illustration—how lucky I've been to have your work on my books. You are such a special artist.

A special shout-out to the educators and librarians and booksellers who have been helping my books find readers for so many years, and to you, the reader, for spending time in my stories.

And of course a big thank-you to my supportive friends and family who show up over and over again in amazing ways. And most of all to Frank, Fia, and Thisbe, who make writing possible, meaningful, and fun. (And this time, an extra helping of gratitude to Fia, who talked through the story with me a hundred times on her walk to kindergarten, and who knew who the villain was long before I did.)